**"You see them ever
nobody ever really notices them."**

Newspaper reporter Jack Richardson is assigned to report on a murder trial, in which twenty year-old Jaylon Soji is accused of the brutal and frenzied killing of a teenager.

Attending the trial, and meeting Jaylon himself, Jack becomes convinced of the boy's innocence, and is determined to prove this.

Then Jaylon changes his plea to guilty…

Philip Cox was born and raised in the UK seaside city of Southend on Sea, which lies forty miles east of London. After graduating from High School, he began a career in UK Banking and Financial Services, and spent the next decades working his way through the ranks, finally becoming a Branch Manager of a major UK bank.

Philip left banking after the birth of his first child to be a stay-at-home father, and it was during this time that, in between changing diapers/nappies, he began to write his first novel, 'After the Rain'.

Now having written fifteen books, he is based in Hertfordshire, some twenty miles north of London, with his wife, two daughters, and three cats.

During his spare time (what spare time there is between school runs and writing!), Philip enjoys indulging his interest in Model Railroading/Railways.

He is tall and slim, has a few grey hairs, and wishes he could get to the gym more often.

www.booksbyphilipcox.com
twitter @philipcoxbooks
www.instagram.com/philipcoxbooks
www.facebook.com/philipcoxbooks

Also by Philip Cox

Detective Sam Leroy
Last to Die
Wrong Time to Die
No Place to Die
Another Way to Die
Ready to Die
No Reason to Die

Jack Richardson
The Value of Nothing
The Angel
The Coyote
The Trail

Standalone thrillers
After the Rain
Dark Eyes of London
She's Not Coming Home
Should Have Looked Away

TWO KINDS OF GUILT

PHILIP COX

This book is copyright material and must not be copied, reproduced, transferred, distributed, leased, licensed or publicly performed or used in any way except as specifically permitted in writing, as allowed under the terms and conditions under which it was purchased or as strictly permitted by applicable copyright law. Any unauthorized distribution or use of this text may be a direct infringement of the author's rights and those responsible may be liable in law accordingly.

Copyright © Philip Cox 2024

Philip Cox has asserted his right under the Copyright, Designs and Patents Act 1988 to be identified as the author of this work.

This book is a work of fiction. Names and characters are the product of the author's imagination and any resemblance to actual persons, living or dead, is entirely coincidental.

www.booksbyphilipcox.com

ISBN 979-8328977388

ACKNOWLEDGEMENTS

All I did was write the book! As always, other people helped in the process. I want to thank, as ever, Anne Poole; the managers and staff at Homerton University Hospital and HM Prison Pentonville; the Metropolitan Police Service for the gang-related information; the residents of Warburton House; and finally, those two individuals I met in Enfield once, who contributed more than they expected to this book.

Cover photograph by Jerry Clack

After his injury, Jack Richardson is forced to make use of some of London's Underground system. Readers unfamiliar with the tube might want to check out a system map on www.tfl.com or check out an A-Z.

There are references to another London newspaper, *The Standard* (London Evening Standard). Between this book being written and published, *The Standard* changed its publication pattern to a weekly print edition, the online edition being daily. The price of progress, I suppose.

All of the events and characters in this book come, as they say, "from the author's imagination". The only exception to this is the deviant sexual practice mentioned in Chapter 14, which I did not make up, neither have I practised it! I stumbled across it while researching my previous book, and held the concept over for this one.

I wonder how many people have gone straight to that chapter?

AS ALWAYS,

FOR ALISON, ELLA AND IONA

CHAPTER ONE

JACK RICHARDSON CARRIED out a word count.

2728.

Almost there.

The article he was working on was meant to be of approximately three thousand words. About two pages. Allowing for the two bar charts he would include, plus three or four photographs he had prepared, it would just fit into the allotted space.

He rubbed his eyes and pinched the top of his nose. He was starting to lose concentration. He had been on this piece all day, since eight that morning: now it was eleven hours later, and he was almost there. He had spent until one o'clock out and about, talking to members of the public, and got back home just before two, and had been working on the article since then. Nothing to eat since a corned beef sandwich from a petrol station at noon. Six cups of black coffee, though. Plus the two Mars Bars during the afternoon.

He stood up from his desk, stretched and made himself another coffee. Strong, black and sweet. There was one Mars Bar left out of the multipack he bought with the petrol earlier. He ate that: not healthy, he knew, but tasty and filling for now. Jack liked chocolate. He would get himself a proper meal when he had completed the article: a proper meal being either something delivered, or something in the microwave.

He returned to his desk. Up until a few months earlier, when he was working from home, which was getting more and more frequent, he would sit at his dining table. Then he read an article about work/life balance, which said that by using furniture and facilities from the home, which were intended as part of the home, part of the non-work life, the job was taking over one's life. One of the recommendations was a dedicated work space, a kind of office at home, which would only be used for work, thereby keeping a virtual barrier between work and personal. Jack could see the logic in this; unfortunately, the size of his two-bedroomed flat prevented this - the second bedroom was kept as a bedroom for when his daughter came to stay - and so a compromise was squeezing a small desk and office chair in one corner of his living room. He kept this only for work, and no work stuff got anywhere near the dining table. Did this arrangement improve Jack's quality of life? The jury was still out on that.

The article Jack was working on was on the subject of corruption in Local Authorities, centred around London, but giving a nationwide overview.

The catalyst for this assignment was the arrest of a number of builders and officials at a London Borough. The builders had been bribing the officials to issue consents for newly constructed buildings where the works and materials were substandard, and corners were cut in the construction. Procedures relating to fire resistance were also circumvented.

Less than two years after completion of one of the buildings, a portion of the outside cladding failed, and the owner of one of the apartments engaged an independent surveyor, and as a result of this surveyor's findings, the extent of the substandard work was revealed.

Another case Jack unearthed was of a manager at a council in the Midlands who was jailed the previous year for claiming over £100,000 in vouchers from a charity scheme to help children living in poverty.

A senior official of a Cornish council was charged at the beginning of the year with the theft of a quarter of a million pounds to spend on laptops, iPads and mobile phones for himself and his family.

There were others.

Jack had obtained a quotation from a lawyer prosecuting one of the cases: she said that there was an alarming lack of government oversight and that local authorities were basically just left to get on with it, with little in the way of sanctions to keep authorities in check. A central government spokesman had told Jack that the most effective sanction is at the ballot box.

The thrust of what Jack was writing was threefold: the activity that was taking place; the lack of oversight and control, and central government apathy.

He was just putting together the final paragraphs when his phone rang. He groaned when he saw who was calling.

'Hey, Mike,' he said, as breezily as possible. Mike Smith was the *London Daily News* news editor, and Jack's supervisor. Jack had always considered him an idiot. 'Just finishing off the corruption piece. I'll be able to upload it tonight.'

'That's great. How many words?'

'Just under three thousand.'

'That should be enough. If you upload tonight, it's in time for tomorrow's online edition, and Wednesday's print edition.'

'That's what I was working on.'

'Great.' Mike coughed, his way of changing the subject. 'Jack, what experience do you have of gangs?'

'As a member of one, or writing about them?'

'I meant in a professional capacity, but... Anyway, Martin is wanting us to have a piece, maybe a series, about London's gang culture.'

'I didn't realise we had a gang culture. Not in a significant way, that is.'

'You might be wrong there, Jack. I won't bore you with the statistics on what the percentage of certain crimes is gang related, but Martin might have something there. He wants us to get something out there before the *Standard* or the nationals do.'

'So that's my next job, is it?'

'I've got some background stuff I'm going to send over for you to look at. Finish the piece you're on first, though. Once that's uploaded, take a look at what I'm sending.'

'Will it keep to the morning?'

'It will, but the court case starts at eleven thirty in the morning.'

'Court case?'

'Yeah. A gang member's been charged with murder. Apparently, he knifed a teenager, who is supposed to be a member of a rival gang.'

'Knifed?'

'Yeah, half a dozen times in the chest. Then slit his throat for good measure.'

'Jesus.'

'Yeah. So, I want you to go to the hearing and take it from there. You know the sort of thing.'

'Okay, I've nearly done the corruption thing. I'll read through the stuff on the gangs when it comes through. Which court, by the way?'

'The Old Bailey, Jack.'

'Okay,' Jack said again. 'Not been there in a while.'

'It's the obvious venue. It's a murder case, Jack.'

CHAPTER TWO

ON THE VERY edge of the City of London – *City* (big C) in the historical and ceremonial sense, not *city* (small c) in the geographical context - running between the thoroughfares of Ludgate Hill and Newgate Street, is a street called Old Bailey. It follows the route of the ancient wall around the City of London, and was part of the fortification's outer wall, or *bailey*.

The street houses the Central Criminal Court of England and Wales, known colloquially and metonymically as the Old Bailey.

The court has been accommodated in a succession of buildings on Old Bailey since the sixteenth century, when it was attached to the medieval Newgate Prison. The current main building was constructed at the beginning of the twentieth century, with an extension over the site of the prison, which was demolished two years later.

The Crown Court sitting here hears major criminal cases from London; occasionally, trials are referred here from other parts of England and Wales. Northern Ireland and Scotland have their own legal systems and court networks.

On the dome above the building stands the symbolic gilt bronze statue of Lady Justice, by the sculptor Pomeroy. Made in 1906, she holds a sword in her right hand and the scales of justice in her left. The statue is supposed to signify blind justice, although the figure is not blindfolded: when sculpted, it was felt her 'maidenly form' guaranteed her impartiality which renders the blindfold redundant.

The building suffered extensive damage during the Blitz; reopened ten years later, the hall underneath the dome displays a series of maxims, such as *the law of the wise is the fountain of life* and *Moses gave unto the people the laws of God.*

The courts have seen many famous trials: Hawley Harvey Crippen, the Kray Twins, the Yorkshire Ripper, and Ruth Ellis, the nightclub hostess who would be the last woman to be hanged, are just a few who have graced the dock of Court Number One, the seats of which are imprinted with the words *Domine, Dirige Nos*, translated as *Lord, direct us*, or *God help us*, depending on whether one is arriving in court from the main entrance or from the cells.

Jack had been told the case was due to begin at eleven thirty that morning. Almost an hour after he had ended the conversation with Mike Smith, the email with details of the assignment arrived. The attachment didn't actually contain much background information, but Jack did notice that the case was due to begin at ten thirty.

The erroneous start time for the case was not all: from what he had been told, Jack was expecting more than what he got. The folder contained one Word document which gave him very little information, so on the train down to the City, Jack checked the Old Bailey website for information.

The case in question was taking place in Court 8. Jaylon (also known as Junior) Soji, 20, of Seven Kings, East London, was accused of the murder of 19 year-old Navindra Dhabi, from Hackney, E8, who was found in a stairwell of a block of flats on the Ashridge Estate with multiple stab wounds to the chest. His throat was also slit. From what Mike Smith had said last night, the victim and the accused were members of rival gangs, and the victim's body was found shortly after a battle on London Fields.

Jack knew from previous visits to the Old Bailey that electronic devices were not allowed into the public areas of the Court: as he had done on previous occasions, he left his phone and portable charger at the dry cleaners at the station. Once he had deposited his items and paid the two pounds charge, he slipped the ticket into his wallet, and walked along Ludgate Hill for the next fifty yards, then making a left into Old Bailey, the street.

The entrance to the building is in Newgate Street, just along from the wide gated archway through which the prison vans arrive with the defendants. However, as he was headed for the public viewing gallery, and not the court itself, Jack turned into Warwick Passage, a short tunnel leading from the street. Halfway down the tunnel, there is a brown door, behind which a flight of stairs leads to the point where two security guards guided Jack through an airport-style walk-through detector.

Once these formalities were done, Jack climbed the stairs to the second landing where the gallery for Court 8 was situated. Jack confirmed to the official that he was aware of the rules regarding the public gallery, and was let in. There were two rows of ten seats, and Jack picked a seat in the centre of the back row. A white middle aged woman sat at the end of the back row, and two much younger, black men were in the middle of the front row. They looked round as Jack sat down.

It looked as if the trial was about to start, as everybody except the defendant was in their places. The judge, a fifty-something woman in black robes, sat at her bench, the Court Clerk directly in front of her. Next were the prosecution and defence barristers; the figures behind them Jack presumed were a solicitor behind the defence barrister, and a junior barrister behind his prosecution counterpart. Jack had been told once that it costs £150 a minute to run a trial here: with the number of officials present, he was surprised it was not more. The dock, separated from the rest of the room by glass screens, was empty.

The twelve members of the jury were also already in place; five women, seven men, a variety of ethnic backgrounds and ages.

One thing which Jack always felt looked out of place here and in any other court for that matter, was how incongruous the technology was in contrast with the classic oak panelling and décor. There were four flat screen monitors dotted around the court, including one facing the dock. Each desk, including the judge's bench, had a flat screen monitor standing on it, sharing space on the other tables with the barristers' laptops. Each pair of jury members also shared a screen. Wires were trailing across each desk, taped down with black tape as they ran to the floor. It amused Jack that even the judge had a white four-socket adaptor on her bench, resting behind her screen and laptop.

After Jack had been sitting in silence for a couple of minutes, the door to the dock opened, and the defendant came out, accompanied by a male custody officer. Jack leaned forward to get a better look at the accused.

He was tall – at least six six, Jack estimated – and stocky. Jack felt his size belied the fact that he was only twenty years old. He was wearing a dark blue jacket, grey trousers, with a white shirt and dark tie. That type of dress did not suit him, Jack felt. His tie was not done up properly. He sat on the chair, with the custody officer behind him, and stared ahead. The two men in the row in front of Jack leaned forward.

Once the court was settled, the judge looked up from the large ring binder on her desk and addressed the defence barrister.

'Mr Carmichael, before we begin the proceedings, I understand you need to address the

Court.'

Carmichael stood and cleared his throat. 'Yes, indeed, My Lady. The defendant wishes to submit a change of plea.'

'To one of guilty, I presume?'

Carmichael nodded. 'Yes, My Lady.'

She took off her glasses before speaking.

'Is this a straightforward guilty plea? Or is the defendant pleading guilty on a proposed basis?' Pleading guilty on a proposed basis is where the defendant admits their guilt, but contends that the allegations made by the prosecution are not accurate or are more serious than what actually happened. Also known as a basis of plea, the defendant will set out their version of events and to what they are pleading guilty. If the prosecution does not accept this and the judge is of the opinion that there is a significant difference between both versions of events, a mini trial, also known as a Newton Hearing, will take place to decide on the facts.

'A straightforward guilty plea, My Lady.'

'Very well.' She put her glasses back on. 'For the record, the defendant needs to stand and make the plea in person.'

After a brief prompt by the custody officer, Jaylon Soji got to his feet.

'Jaylon Soji,' the judge asked, her eyes alternating from her notes and the dock, 'do you plead guilty to the premeditated murder of Navindra Dhabi?'

The defendant swallowed, and replied, quietly. 'Guilty.' He then sat down, prompted by the custody officer.

The judge swung her chair forty-five degrees towards the jury.

'Ladies and gentleman,' she said, 'for you this is an unexpected although I suspect not unwelcome development. Before I discharge you, I would like to thank you all for the time you have spent here so far.' She swung back to address the defence barrister. 'In the light of the change of plea a criminal trial is no longer required. I propose now to adjourn to fully consider the facts of this case and review the reports that have been prepared so I can make an informed decision before I pass sentence. We will adjourn until…' She looked down at some papers on her bench. 'The twenty-fifth.'

The judge rose, the members of the court doing likewise until she had left. The two men in the row in front began whispering. Jack was still leaning forward and found himself staring at the figure in the dock. As he did so, the defendant looked up at him. At first, Jack assumed he was looking at the other two men, but then realised he was staring at him. Their eyes met, and Jack saw not a murderer, but somebody who was barely an adult. Not somebody who had stabbed a contemporary multiple times and cut his throat, but a very frightened and overwhelmed twenty year-old.

Scared and confused.

CHAPTER THREE

JACK RETRIEVED HIS phone and charger from the store at the station and called Mike Smith, updating him with what had happened in Court that morning. He could hear his News Editor exhale loudly.

'Shit. It could have been a really juicy story, something for the readers to enjoy.'

'Yeah, could've been,' Jack agreed.

'So there's not going to be a trial. Has he been sentenced?'

'No, the case has been adjourned for around three weeks for reports. But the thing is, Mike…'

'What?'

Jack was going to tell Mike about how he felt when Soji looked up at him from the dock, but decided against it. He had been down this type of road before. He bluffed instead. 'I was going to say, even though there won't be a trial, the details of the murder are still the same, and if you and Martin are right, and this is the consequence of gang warfare, then there's still plenty to write about, wouldn't you say?'

'What do you have in mind?'

'For a start, pieces on him, and the victim. Human interest; their backstories. They're both around the same age, same backgrounds, maybe. If they've both been dragged into gang culture, then they're both victims.'

'I wouldn't paint the killer into some sort of victim when, what was it? Six stab wounds to the chest and one across the throat? Not exactly the work of a victim.'

'I obviously can't paint him the same way as the boy who was killed, but there was obviously a reason why he was over at London Fields that night.'

'There's the matter of County Lines.'

'In what way, Mike?'

'You've heard of the County Lines?'

'Of course I have, but I don't see the connection here.'

County Lines is where illegal drugs are

transported from one area to the other, across local authority and police force boundaries. This transportation is normally, though not totally, carried out by children or vulnerable people who are strongarmed into it by gangs. The so-called *County Line* is the mobile phone line used to take orders for the drugs, a *deal line*. Methods of coercion include intimidation, violence, including sexual violence, and weapons. The dealers frequently target these vulnerable adults or children to act as the mules or to move cash so that they themselves can stay under the law enforcement radar. The vulnerable adults frequently have addiction or mental health problems. In some cases, the dealers will take over the vulnerable person's home, and use it as a base. This is known as cuckooing. People in these situations are often exposed to physical, mental and sexual abuse, and in some cases are trafficked away from home as part of the drug dealing business. Where children are used, they often fail to see themselves as victims or realise they are being groomed to get involved.

'The killer and the deceased were both members of gangs, weren't they?'

'They were, but if we're talking County Lines, it's individuals who are recruited. It's not gang warfare; it's far more subtle than that. Not an out and out brawl in the middle of East London on a

Friday night.'

There was a pause. Jack could tell Mike was thinking through what he had just said. Eventually, 'You might be right there; I get what you're saying.' Another pause for thought. 'Why not just centre your piece on the two kids concerned?'

'That's what I was thinking.' *That's what I was going to do all along, you idiot.* 'Some background to their home life, families, how they got involved in their respective gangs. Was it voluntary, because there was nothing else to do? Or were they forced into it; peer pressure, I mean.'

'The dead boy *and* his killer?'

'Yeah. Both sides of the coin.'

'A comparison?'

'Not exactly. Two stories, running side by side. Then meeting with tragic consequences. They were both around the same age, nineteen and twenty: I'll try and talk to their parents, to Soji himself.'

'Where will he be?'

'I'll have to check. Belmarsh, maybe. He's been charged with murder, after all. It would have to be a Category A prison. What's nearby? The Scrubs?'

'He was East London, that right?'

'Both were. The victim was from London

Fields, where he was killed, and Soji was from Seven Kings.'

Mike said, 'Two rival gangs.' Then there was silence. Jack knew he was thinking. Then, 'Sounds like it could be a feature, or a short series, about London gang culture. Do you know how many gangs there are in the city?'

'I can only guess; this is the first time I've had a story like this.'

'I think we're talking three figures, Jack.'

'Look, Mike: I don't want to get ahead of myself here. My starting point is these two kids. Let's see where that leads, yes?'

'Okay. Keep me up to date, then.'

With a sigh of relief, Jack ended the call. There being nothing to do where he was, Jack decided to get back up home, get online, and begin researching his story. The paper's archives might have something to get him started. Then he would reach out to Navindra Dhabi's family to get some background there. That would mean a trip to London Fields. Then the same with Jaylon Soji, which would mean a trip to Seven Kings. He would also need to talk with some of the gang members: that would be difficult. He would need to identify them first, and that would be a challenge: they would hardly have a Head Office or a website.

He got back on his train. Sitting on a long

longitudinal seat, he stared at the other side of the carriage. The train had gone into a tunnel, and he could see his own reflection in the glass opposite. Then he could see Jaylon Soji's face staring at him.

That expression: panic? Bewilderment? Confusion?

Or a cry for help?

CHAPTER FOUR

ONCE HE HAD got back home, Jack fixed himself a sandwich and booted up his laptop. He headed first to the paper's online archive, and searched for gangs in London. Had that search not been successful, then he would have gone on to other papers' records. As it happened, what he found in the *Daily News* archive, he felt was sufficient for his purposes.

He found himself going back to the turn of the century, which seemed an appropriate starting point. There was not exactly a plethora of articles, but on average two or three a year. In most cases, the gang was incidental: the article was not about gangs *per se*, rather about a crime - murder, assault, robbery – and gang membership was seen as being a factor.

Whilst not directly related to any particular incident, in 2007 there were several articles, and Letters to the Editor. Jack learned that there had been a BBC documentary in February of that year, putting the facts in the public eye, at least until the next big issue cropped up.

It was estimated at that time that there were 169 separate gangs. Jack thought it puzzling that they could be so precise. Of that 169, more than twenty-five percent were said to be involved in murders. Further down this article, which got the figure from a police report, Jack read that several London Boroughs questioned the accuracy as the existence of certain gangs on the list could not be verified.

Another article, some weeks later, quoted a criminologist as saying that there were probably no more than fifteen hundred to two thousand young people in gangs all over London, but their impact was said to be enormous. The piece did admit there was a lack of methodology and evidence for this figure, which to Jack seemed very high, even in a city where there are just over two million inhabitants between the ages of ten and thirty.

A third piece that year reported that the

dominant gang at that time, which was based in Southall, boasted 2500 members, and stated that, using the same methodology as is used by American gang experts, six percent of people in the ten to nineteen age range were classified as belonging to a gang. As far as ethnicity was concerned, 78% of gang members were said to be Black, 13% White, 6.5% Asian, 2.2% Middle Eastern or Arab, and under 1% East Asian. Jack knew a little about socio-economics and so was not surprised at this breakdown.

From six years ago he found something he was looking for and which clicked in his mind as it was familiar to what he had read on the Jaylon Soji case notes Mike had forwarded to him.

He read that London gangs mark their territory with gang graffiti: no surprise there, he thought; but there was a trend to use the post code area or housing estate they identify with. Jack checked on the assignment notes: Jaylon Soji was allegedly a member of a gang named THE KINGS, and hailed from Seven Kings. That made sense. By the same token, Navindra Dhabi, the victim, lived in London Fields, which is London E8. He checked the list he had of known gangs in London. There was one called THE E8 GANG. Jack leaned back against the back of the chair and pinched the bridge of his nose.

The murder took place during a gang fight.

Now, was the victim a gang member also, not just an innocent bystander? Not to deny Soji's guilt, but maybe things weren't as clear cut as he first thought. He stretched, returned to his screen and read on.

In many cases, the gang will tag the street road signs with their gang colour or logo; the article gave some examples, none of which were in the E8 area. Whilst apparently not a recent phenomenon, it had become a more integrated part of the gang culture. Many gangs have a strong sense of belonging to their local areas and often take their names from the housing estates and postcode areas where they are located. In some cases, the postcode acts as a boundary between rival gang territory, although there are known to be rival gangs operating out of the same postcode areas well as gangs which occupy more than one area.

A piece in the archive from four years back said that researchers found that gangs in a north-east borough of London which used to be organised around postcode rivalries had moved from disputes around boundaries to focus on profit-making activities like drug dealing. This development apparently follows a well-established gang evolution model, which details how gangs progress from recreational goals and activities like defending territory to financial goals and activities like protection rackets and drug dealing. There was a quotation that some gangs resemble not just crime that is organised, but organised crime. Some gangs in London use hand signs and tattoos to signify membership; some are motivated by religion, but profits arising from drugs and other criminal activity are a significant motivator for many gangs, around sixty percent.

Whilst predominately based in West London coded areas, Asian drug gangs have also figured, with Turkey replacing Pakistan and Afghanistan as the most important transit point for heroin. Eighty percent of heroin intercepted in the United Kingdom belongs to Turkish gangs. A number of murders in London fifteen years ago were said to have been linked to a heroin drugs war between rival Turkish and Kurdish gangs in North London. The authorities believed the feud was between two organised drug gangs, one based in Tottenham, the other in Hackney. Jack rubbed his chin: there was E8 again. The Hackney gang's leader was convicted and jailed. Who or what took his place, Jack wondered.

He pushed the laptop away and scanned the notes he had made. He got up and took his plate and coffee mug into the kitchen, and as he washed them, he tried to form a picture of what was going on with Jaylon Soji. A member perhaps of the gang from Seven Kings. They make a trip to Hackney: was this journey just for a fight, or was it for something else? Did they go because that was just what gangs do? Somewhere along the line, he meets up with Navindra Dhabi, who could be a member of the local gang. And somewhere further along the line, he kills him. But did Soji look like a killer? Not standing in the dock that morning, he didn't.

And all this stuff Jack had gleaned about organised crime and drugs: was that relevant to what he had here?

He decided he needed to do some ground work. Not today: by the time he got to Seven Kings or even Hackney, it would be getting dark.

He would go in the morning.

CHAPTER FIVE

ONCE HE HAD allowed enough time for the rush hour to have passed, Jack set off in the car for Seven Kings. He left home at nine thirty, and arrived just before eleven. He took the North Circular as far as Ilford, then transferred to the A118 trunk road. Not Jack's ideal route, but better than the alternative one.

Before he left he tried looking up an address in the telephone directory. It was worth a shot. He found three entries for Soji. One was in Southall, West London and the second was in Croydon, South London. He dismissed both of these, but the third was to the East, in Goodmayes, which is very close to Seven Kings.

On arrival, he found a space in the large retail park in the centre of the town, outside a supermarket. He called the Goodmayes number. A man's voice answered. Young-sounding, with an accent.

'Could I speak to Mr or Mrs Soji, please?' Jack asked politely.

'My father no longer lives here,' came the reply. Jack detected a note of anger in the voice. 'My mother is in. Who wants to talk to her?'

Jack introduced himself.

'We don't want to talk to any newspapers. Just leave us alone!'

Jack tried to answer. 'But…' The other person had hung up. Jack wasn't really surprised. 'Shit,' he said, tossing the phone down onto the passenger seat. He had the address; he should have just gone round there.

Which is what he did. The road was not far from the retail park, and even after two red lights, he got there in five minutes. He drove slowly down the road, looking for the house number. Vehicles were parked on both sides of the street, but he was the only car travelling, so he was able to keep to fifteen or twenty miles per hour, looking out at the house numbers. Somehow, the houses were not what he had expected. They were large, albeit terraced, houses, 1900s, four bedrooms, two reception rooms, he suspected. Most of the houses had had their front gardens converted to full width driveways, some having two cars parked side by side. Not the type of area he would have expected a murder suspect to have come from, although he had been told many times about the danger of making generalisations.

However, as he got further down the road, things changed. The buildings were still 1900s four bedroomed, two receptioned, terraced houses, with periodic end of terraced dwellings, but as he got further down the road the appearance of the houses slowly changed. Less well-maintained, some even shabby. Older cars on the driveways; where there was a garden, more often than not, the lawns had not seen a mower in months, fences had collapsed, black wheelie bins proliferated, invariably surrounded by full bin bags.

He eventually came across the house number he was looking for, and got a parking space across the road, five doors down. The full width driveway had once been brick-paved, but in an almost semicircular shape around the front step and door, it looks as if somebody had tried to remove the bricks, leaving a cemented base. The upstairs curtains were drawn, and the nets at the front ground floor were at a forty-five degree angle, a hook having failed. There was a motorbike against the far fence, covered by a dirty grey tarpaulin. On the other side, near the front door, two black rubbish bags rested against the wall. A flowerbed ran the length of the garden: it showed signs of having been cultivated, plants every two feet or so, but these were now almost overwhelmed by weeds. To the left of the front door stood an ornate pedestal, weather-stained, and containing a dead plant. The wooden front door was black, paint peeling off at various points.

Jack noticed at this point that the house had been converted into flats. There was an intercom, and two doorbells, with the corresponding numbers crudely painted onto the brickwork: 23 and 23A. He remembered from the directory that it was definitely 23, no A.

He rang the bell.

No answer.

He waited ten seconds, then rang again, putting his ear to the glass on the door to check if he could hear anything, a faint ring, maybe. Nothing.

Then came a reply. Indistinct, but that was probably poor quality intercom wiring.

A woman's voice. 'Yes?'

Jack put his mouth to the speaker. 'I rang earlier.'

'Leave us alone. We have nothing to say. My

son never killed anyone.'

'I know he didn't,' Jack said. 'That's why I need to see…'

There was a click as the door unlocked. Jack pushed the door open and walked into a small lobby. It was obvious that when the house was converted into flats, a wooden partition was constructed at the foot of the stairs, with two doors, 23A leading upstairs, and 23 leading to the ground floor flat.

The thought entered Jack's head that he was arguably entering under false pretences, as he did not know that Jaylon Soji didn't kill anyone, but now he had gotten so far, he would have to bluff.

The cream coloured door opened. Jack noticed there was a dark scuff mark lower down on the door, as if somebody had tried to kick their way in. A tall, skinny black man stood in the doorway. Jack took him for mid-twenties. He wore a bright green tee shirt, and brown long shorts, bare sandalled feet. 'Mum says to come in,' he said.

Jack followed the man down the hall, making sure he closed the door behind. He was being led to the back of the house; the kitchen, as Jack could smell food being cooked. It smelt spicy, but he couldn't place what it was.

A woman Jack took as being Mrs Soji, Jaylon's mother, was at the stove, stirring something in a large saucepan.

'Come in, sit down,' she said in a quiet voice. 'Would you like some tea?'

'No, thank you,' Jack said as he sat at the kitchen table.

'Don't think me impolite,' she said. 'I would normally join you at the table for tea, but I need to keep stirring this *Matumbu*, or it will burn to the pan. If Jamal,' she said, nodding over to her son, 'was a girl, he'd be doing this.'

'Don't worry. It smells very nice, by the way.'

'I've seen you before,' Jamal said, pointing at Jack. 'You were at the court. You were sitting in the public gallery.'

'In the row behind you. I thought your face seemed familiar.'

'Is that right?' she asked. 'You were there?'

'Yes, I was.'

'I didn't go,' she said sadly, stirring all the time. It was if she was talking to the food; she made no eye contact with Jack. 'I should have gone, I know, but I was so angry with Junior.'

'Junior?' Jack asked.

'Our family name for Jaylon. He's three years younger than Jamal. They're all I have now...' She paused a second. 'I was so annoyed with him for changing his plea to guilty.'

'He pled not guilty originally?' asked Jack.

'Of course. He didn't do it. I told the police he didn't do it.'

'But the police must have had evidence. I haven't seen the full details yet, but...'

'They found him there,' said Jamal angrily. 'His fingerprints were on the knife, they found that kid's blood on his hands, on his clothes. He's an idiot!'

'Jamal!' shouted his mother. 'Stop that! Go to the shops or something. Go get me some coconut milk for this.'

Grabbing a brown leather jacket off the back of a chair, Jamal said, 'All right, Mama. But think about the other boy's blood on Junior's hands, and trousers, and... What's the use?' He left, slamming the door behind him.

Mrs Soji paused a beat, then said to Jack, 'I'm sorry about that, but Jamal is very upset. He and Junior are very close, but he thinks his brother did it.'

'And you don't think he did?'

'Of course not, Mr....?'

'Richardson.'

'Mr Richardson. I'm his mother. Do you have any children?'

'Yes, I have a teenage daughter.'

'And if she was arrested for murder, would you accept that she was guilty?'

Jack shook his head slowly. 'Of course not.'

Mrs Soji stopped stirring. She moved the pan off the gas ring and turned off the gas. She rinsed her hands at the sink, dried them, and joined Jack at the table.

'Now, Mr Richardson,' she said. 'You said that you didn't believe my son killed that boy either. So what do you need to prove he is innocent?'

Jack swallowed.

CHAPTER SIX

HE DECIDED TO bluff. She seemed like a nice lady, one who was in an invidious position as one of her sons was on trial for murder, and he felt guilty. Guilty for the subterfuge and for being economical with the truth with her, but he needed to speak with her to get material for his piece.

'I need to find out more about Jaylon,' he said.

'He is twenty years old,' she began. 'He is my youngest son. Jamal is my other son; he is older. Jaylon was born here, in this house. He went to school here, ten minutes' walk away to begin with, then a short bus ride away.'

'Is his father here also?'

She shook her head. 'None of us has seen his father for over fifteen years.' She paused a second and took a deep breath, putting her hands, which had been resting on her lap, onto the table. 'Let me show you his room.'

Jack nodded and stood up with her, then let her lead him out of the kitchen, down the narrow hallway to a room at the back of the house.

The room was tidy and uncluttered, not what one would expect from a twenty year-old boy, although Jack made the assumption that his mother was responsible for the state of the room.

Definitely not the room of a typical twenty year-old: the single bed was neatly made, the duvet cover with images of guitars and matching pillow were smoothed down. A Yamaha classical guitar rested in the corner of the room, propped up against the wall. Jack looked around the room. The walls were painted a shade of light grey, pristine: on the walls were four A3 sized posters: two of the *One Direction* group; the other two were of the singers Harry Styles and Justin Bieber. Not what one would expect of a twenty year-old boy, he thought; then corrected himself, as this was really the room of a twenty year-old man.

Against the wall opposite the bed was a white desk - probably Ikea – and around the desk, in some cases hanging from the ceiling on wires, was a collection of plastic kits, assembled, and painted.

Jack raised his eyebrows. 'Airfix?' he asked Mrs Soji.

She shrugged her shoulders. 'He loves making these. Spends all his time working on them.'

Jack stepped over and took a closer look. Hanging from the ceiling were a helicopter and an RAF fighter jet: Jack recognised the helicopter as a Westland but could not identify the jet. On the desk, against the wall, were models of a 19th century paddle steamer, the Titanic, and the German battleship Bismarck. He easily recognised the Titanic and recalled assembling a model of the Bismarck when he was a boy – around eight or nine, though, not twenty. However, he could not help being impressed by the quality of the models, beautifully assembled and painted, the decals exquisitely applied.

He turned to Jaylon's mother. 'These are fantastic. This is how he spends his evenings?'

'This is how he spends his days.'

'Oh? He doesn't...'

'He doesn't have a job. He went to college after he left school, but had problems with some of the other students. He's had two or three jobs since then – shop work – but none of them worked out.'

'So he spends his time on these models?

They're beautiful.'

She nodded over to the guitar. 'Or on his guitar. He likes to write music, write songs. That's what he went to college for, to study music, but…'

Jack said nothing; just nodded and studied the models.

'My Jaylon isn't like boys his age.'

Jack looked up from examining the detail on the Westland. 'In what way, Mrs Soji?'

'He's always been a bit different. He's always preferred his own company, he doesn't seem to relate to strangers.'

'These models are so good. He obviously has a talent there.'

'He has others – in the cupboard over there. I think those ones you can see are the most recent ones. I think there are some boxes under his bed of models he hasn't put together yet.'

'What about his brother? Is he the same?'

'No, Jamal is totally different. He's older, for a start. He has a job – the same one – for two or three years. He delivers food on his motorbike. He has friends too.'

'Girlfriends?'

'One or two. He had a very nice one last year. A very nice white girl, but nothing came of it. I think he's too young for that anyway – he needs to do things, get experiences, travel. I had him when I was twenty-three: sometimes I wish I'd waited a bit longer, but his father... I didn't mean... Oh, that sounded terrible.'

'No, it doesn't. I totally agree with you. I think if you settle down too young, there are a lot of things you miss out on, things to do, places to go, that you never get the chance to do in later life. My sister had her daughter when she was around your son's age, and in later years she resented the fact that she'd missed out in her younger years. So, unlike his brother, Jamal has lots of friends. Is he in a gang?'

'He's in a group of friends.' She smiled. 'They call themselves *The Kings*, because they're all from around Seven Kings.'

'I see,' said Jack. Something was beginning to fit in place. 'Did Jaylon ever go out with Jamal? With this group, I mean.'

'Jamal took him once or twice, but only because I asked him to. I don't think he really wanted to. He was out with him the night that poor boy got stabbed. But there was no way my son would have done it.'

'Can you tell me about that night?'

She sat on the bed. 'Jaylon was in here. It was after we had eaten, and Jamal said he was going to go out and meet up with his Kings group. I said why not take your brother with you; he'd been in here on his own all day. Jamal said he would. I could tell he didn't want to though; there was a lot of huffing and puffing. I don't think Jaylon was that keen, either, but he went along with it.'

'And can you remember what time they went out?'

'It must have been around seven o'clock. We had just finished dinner, and I was doing the dishes.'

'And what happened later?'

'I think it was around midnight. I usually stay up if Jamal is out, and I must have fallen asleep in my chair. I heard the doorbell, and I got up, thinking it was the boys, that they had left their door key behind. But it wasn't: it was three police officers. One in uniform and two detectives. One was a woman. The older detective, the man, said that Jaylon had been arrested over at London Fields on suspicion of murder. He had a piece of paper in his hand which he said was a search warrant so they could search Jaylon's bedroom.'

'So they searched here? I take it they didn't find anything?'

'Nothing at all, of course. They left the place in a mess, though. At least they didn't damage his models. I had to tidy up afterwards, though; although this is how he usually keeps it.'

'Did they search his brother's room?'

'No. Only here. They were only here half an

hour. They told me he was being held at Bethnal Green police station. When I said his father was not around the lady detective asked if I had anybody to call. I said I did – my sister lives not too far from here. Just after they left, I was just about to call my sister when Jamal got home. I asked where they'd been and…'

She was interrupted by Jamal arriving home. 'Let's go back into the kitchen,' she said. Back in the kitchen, Jamal had the fridge door open.

'Oh, he's still here,' he said to his mother. 'Here's the milk, Mama; I need to get off to work now. See you this afternoon.' He brushed past Jack and went back out again.

'He's affected by all this,' she said. 'More than he lets on.'

'That's understandable. You were saying when Jamal got home that night.'

'Oh, yes. He said he and Jaylon met up with their group. Some of them said they were going to get the train over to Hackney to meet up with some friends. Jamal said he didn't want to, so went for something to eat on his own; but a couple of the group were getting friendly with Jaylon and said would he like to go with them.'

'Which he did.'

'Yes. So we got a taxi over to the police station and were told he had been charged with that other boy's murder. They didn't believe me when I said he couldn't have done. And he's been in custody ever since.'

'Where is he being held?'

'In Pentonville.'

'He's got a solicitor?'

'Oh yes, my brother-in-law knew of one, and he's taking care of things. What will happen now that he's pleaded guilty?'

'Nothing until the sentencing hearing.'

'So, can you help?'

'I can put things in the newspaper, that's about it. But I'll need to make a few enquiries myself. I can't make any promises, though.'

She nodded.

'I'll need to talk with his brother,' Jack said.

'That might be difficult. You saw what he is like.'

'I know. I might have more luck away from here, where there's just the two of us. Where does he work? You said he delivers meals on his bike: is that Deliveroo, or something?'

'It might be. I know he delivers pizzas which people have ordered over the phone or over the internet.'

'Pizzas from where?'

'Pizza Cottage. They have a shop opposite the train station.'

'I'll go over there. Thank you for your time, Mrs Soji, and I'll do what I can.'

She thanked him, and said goodbye as she let him out. He walked back to his car. He would head back into the town centre and try to collar Jamal at work. Without his mother around, he might react differently and Jack could be more forceful. As he pulled away and headed up to the High Street, he thought about the stuff in Jaylon's room. The guitar, the music, the exquisite model making. This was somebody who likes his own company and his own world. Jack wondered what Jaylon's issue was, given the interaction difficulties and the solitude, the attention to detail, but decided to park that for now.

The murder victim had been stabbed several times in the chest and had had his throat cut.

Jaylon Soji liked creating things, music, songs, models; all with loving care.

The two didn't seem quite compatible.

CHAPTER SEVEN

IT WAS ALMOST lunchtime, so the pizza store, which was opposite the station in the centre of the High Street, was starting to get busy. It was not an actual restaurant, just premises where pizzas were made to order for collection by customers or for delivery.

Ideally, Jack would have found a parking space nearby from which he could look out for Jamal, but there were none; in any case, the traffic was too busy to get a good view of the store. In the event, he was able to park in the supermarket car park around the corner. It was free for three hours, which would give him plenty of time.

There was a café across the street from the pizza store: it seemed okay, so Jack went inside, bought himself a toasted cheese sandwich and a bottle of water. He found himself a table in the window and got into position. He had just sat down when he saw Jamal come out of the store, holding a black crash helmet and a large blue pizza box. Jack held up his phone and took a picture of Jamal getting on his motorcycle: he thought it would be an idea to get a note of the registration number.

Over the next hour, he noticed, as well as Jamal, three other delivery persons, one more on a motorbike, two with cars. One car had the pizza store logo on the doors. He observed Jamal make three trips, back and forth. The store was obviously popular: as well as the four riders, there was a regular stream of customers calling in for takeaways.

By one thirty, things were beginning to slow down. He noticed Jamal arrive back at the store; when he emerged a minute later, rather than put a delivery box into the pouch on his bike, he paused, hung the helmet on the handle bars, then leaned on the bike to light up a cigarette.

This was Jack's chance. He left the table, nodded a goodbye to the woman on the till, and hurried across the road, weaving in and out of the slow-moving traffic.

As Jack approached, Jamal saw him and recognised him immediately. He mouthed something, tossed his cigarette on the pavement and began to put on his helmet.

'Jamal, can we talk for a few minutes?' Jack asked, breathlessly.

Saying nothing, Jamal finished strapping on his helmet.

'Please,' Jack repeated.

'I told you, I've got nothing to say to you. Fuck off.'

Jack stood in front of the bike. 'Please. Just a few minutes. What have you got to lose? Have you had your lunch yet? Let me buy you lunch.'

Jamal paused. 'Okay. I'm hungry anyway. Buy me lunch.'

'All right. Let's go over to that café. It's good in there. Unless you want pizza.'

Jamal smirked slightly. 'I don't want pizza.' He secured his bike to the lamppost and, holding his crash helmet, walked across the road with Jack. They located a table – a different one, as all the window tables were now taken – and Jack ordered a coffee for himself and a coke with an All Day Breakfast for Jamal. They sat for a few minutes before the food arrived: two fried eggs, two rashers of bacon, two sausages, mushrooms, baked beans, black pudding, and a slice of buttered toast. Jamal attacked the meal as if he had not eaten in weeks.

Jack broke the silence. 'So tell me about your brother. Your mother says he's a bit different to other guys his age.'

Jamal looked up, his mouth stuffed with food. When he had swallowed most of it, he said, 'He's just a bit... retarded.'

'Autistic, you mean? Special needs?'

'I don't know what any of that stuff means.'

Jack tried from another angle. 'Well, what do you mean retarded? How is he retarded?'

'He doesn't understand things. He doesn't relate to people like most guys do. Can't cope with stuff; that's when his temper kicks in. Doesn't have any friends. He couldn't cope with college, and couldn't keep a job for any more than a few weeks. He just sits in his room on his own making those fucking toy planes.'

'They're beautiful models, brilliantly made. He obviously has a skill there.'

Jamal just shrugged.

'Your mother said he's into music as well.'

'He does that, yes. He writes songs, love songs. Fuck knows who to.'

'Do you think he killed that other boy?'

'Had to have done, yeah? They found him at the scene with his prints on the knife and blood all over his clothes. Not his blood, either.'

'What did he say about it?'

'He says he can't remember anything about it. That's bullshit.'

'So what happened that night, then?' asked Jack. 'Your mother said he went out with you and your gang. The Kings? Tell me about The Kings.'

'It's a group of around ten of us, all from around here. We call ourselves that because we're all from here, Seven Kings, get it?'

'I get it, yes. So what do you do in this gang, this group?'

'We just hang out, do shit together. Go to parties.' He leaned forward and half whispered, half mouthed, 'Drugs.' Then he sat back up. 'My mother kept asking me to take Junior with me, said it would be a way of getting him to meet other people.'

'Which you did.'

'Once or twice. Fucking waste of time, if you ask me. That evening, though, one of the guys wanted to go over to Hackney, said he had some business to do with one of the guys over there.'

'That guy would be from the E8 gang? What business was he talking about?'

'Probably. I think he was buying some stuff from one of the E8 dudes. I didn't want to go, I'd already arranged to meet up with a girl I've been seeing. I told Junior to go home, but he had got friendly with a couple of the others. They said they'd look after him. I met up with my girlfriend. We - well, you can guess what we did. I left hers later on, got home around twelve. When I got home the police were already there, searching his room. Didn't find nothing, though. Mum was hysterical, I had to calm her down. Once the cops had left, I had to call my Auntie to come over.'

'There was no trial because he changed his plea at the last minute. Do you know why he would have done that?'

'Your guess is as good as mine. Maybe he realised he'd get a lighter sentence if he admitted it. Do without a trial. Is all this stuff going in your paper? You are a reporter, aren't you? Should you be paying me for all this?'

'Probably. There's no trial to report on, so I'm just checking out some background stuff first. I have a problem with all this, though.'

'A problem?' Jamal laughed. 'Don't we all?'

'My problem's this,' said Jack. 'The other kid - Navindra Dhabi - was stabbed in the chest five or six times. Once would have been enough. And his throat was cut. The first stab would have probably killed him. Why the others? Why slit his throat as well? It was like the person doing it was enjoying it. One stab would have been enough; the others were because his killer enjoyed it. Your brother is very shy, very solitary. He makes beautiful plastic models, he writes music, love songs.

'To me that doesn't sound like a sadistic killer. What do you think?'

Jamal said nothing.

CHAPTER EIGHT

THE CAR REPAIR workshop must have been less than a mile away, but it took Jack twenty minutes to reach it, after sitting in traffic most of the way.

After Jamal had demolished his All Day Breakfast, Jack asked why, if he left early that night, his brother stayed.

'He didn't want to. He was tight with a couple of the other guys. They said they'd look after him, make sure he got home okay.'

'Do these guys have names?'

'One's called Derek – Derek Ajao.'

'Derek Ajao. And the other?'

'I think he's Del's cousin. Don't know his

name.'

'Okay. So where can I find Derek Ajao?'

'He'll be at work now, I guess. Works in a car repair place, not far from here.'

Jack nodded. 'What's this place called?'

'Auto something.'

'Auto something? That's unusual for a car repair place. Auto what?' By now, Jack had taken three ten pound notes from his pack pocket and was holding them in on the table.

'Auto Breeze,' said Jamal. 'That's it: Auto Breeze?'

'Breeze? As in …?' Jack tried to find the right word.

'They do air conditioning. The AC on your car breaks down, you take it there.'

Jack took out his phone and Googled the firm. He found it straightaway. 'I've got it,' he said, then looked up at Jamal. 'Anything else you can tell me?'

'About what?'

'About anything. About that night, about your Kings gang, about your brother? Anything.'

'No, told you all I can,' Jamal replied, his eyes fixed on the ten pound notes Jack was holding.

Jack sighed and slid the money across table. 'That's for your time, and the information.'

'Cheers,' Jamal said as he pocketed the cash. 'I'll be getting off now.'

Jack watched Jamal leave and walk across the road to his bike, then left the café himself to walk back to his car.

Now he was at the repair shop. Almost there, rather, as the establishment was somewhat off the beaten track. The Google search took Jack to around halfway down a residential street, rows of terraced houses down either side. He pulled up to check his bearings; it was then he found he was in the right place after all. Across the road, between two sets of terraces, was a narrow road, only enough space for one vehicle at a time. He stayed parked where he was, and walked over.

It looked as if this road, which looked to be more pothole than tarmac, led to something similar running behind the houses, like an access road between this street and the next. As he got to the end, carefully avoiding the potholes which were filled with rainwater, he saw the car repair shop. The name *Auto Breeze*, was showing on a rusty metal sign fixed above what was no more than a standalone garage, above an open shutter door. There were two rows of vehicles - five cars and a van, three deep – parked in front, and Jack had to squeeze between these to get to the shop. He noticed that one of the cars had a flat tyre.

Squeezing his way through, he came across a man wearing a black coat and matching beanie. He looked in his sixties at least, and had silver hair, reaching a couple of inches below his collar. He was vaping.

'Can I help you?' he asked.

'Yes, I'm looking for Derek,' Jack replied.

'I'll get him.'

The silver haired man went inside and emerged again with a much younger man, taller, white, short hair tinted red and a black earring.

'Yes, mate?' the man said to Jack.

Jack was confused. This could hardly be Derek Ajao.

'Derek Ajao?' he asked, tentatively.

'No, you want Derek, the other Derek. I'll get him. Is it about a car?'

'Not exactly. I'm a friend of the family, sort of. I just needed a quick word.'

This Derek leaned into the shop and called out, 'Derek!'

A much younger, black, man appeared. He was wearing dirty blue overalls and a black beanie matching the other man's. As he walked up to Jack, he was wiping his hands on a rag.

'Don't be too long,' the other Derek called out from inside the workshop.

'Yes?' asked Derek. 'You want to see me?'

'If you've got ten minutes.'

Derek looked back into the workshop. 'Five.' They both stepped out of earshot of the repair shop. 'You the guy from the paper?' he asked.

Jack nodded. 'Jamal called you, did he?'

'Yeah, said you were coming over. You want to ask some questions about his brother?'

'A few, and about what happened that evening.'

'He said you gave him thirty quid.'

'You can have the same, if you can give me the information I need.'

Derek shuffled about. 'Fairs. What you want to know?'

'I'm researching for a piece I'm writing about that murder over in Hackney.'

'Yeah, I know what you're talking about. His brother got arrested for it.'

'Do you think he did it?'

Derek shrugged. 'The law thinks he did.'

'Jamal told me his brother was with you. You and your cousin, was it?'

Derek nodded. 'Yeah?'

'He said he decided to go home, and left Jaylon with you. You said you'd keep an eye on him and see he got home okay.'

'Might have done. But he didn't go home. He went to see some girl he's been seeing.'

'That would figure, as we know he didn't get home till around midnight. But when he had left, Jaylon stayed with you?'

'That's right. He said Jamal was a party pooper for leaving so early.' Derek sniggered.

'Odd kid.'

'Anyway, after his brother left, Jaylon stayed with you.'

'Me and a couple of others, yeah.'

'So what did you do? Where did you go?'

'One of the others said how about going over to Hackney for the night.'

'The evening. Get the night bus back.'

'Go to Hackney to do what?'

'He said -'

'He?'

'One of the others. He said he had some business to do with someone over there.'

'Who? What sort of business?'

'Don't know any names. A dude from over there. Not sure what kind of business he meant. Buying something, I think.'

'Drugs?'

Derek glanced back at the workshop to make sure nobody was in earshot. He shrugged. 'Maybe,' he said, quietly.

Jack lowered his own voice. 'I'll take that as a yes. So, tell me what happened. Jamal left to go and do his own thing. You, with Jaylon and your cousin and the rest of the Kings, went over to Hackney.'

'How'd you know about the Kings?'

Jack shook his head. 'Jamal told me. So did his mother, as it happens. How did you get over there? Drive?'

'No, we took the train. Got off at Hackney Central. We all got off there, started to walk down the main road to where he was supposed to me meeting this other fella. We went into the KFC as we were all hungry, got something to eat. Then we carried on walking down the road, saw a crowd of other guys across the road, on the corner by the Pizza Express. They saw us, and started shouting stuff at us, then it all kicked off.'

'In what way kicked off?'

At that moment, the older Derek called out, 'Del? You done there?'

'I need to go,' Derek said, uneasily.

'Okay, just a couple more questions. They were shouting at you: what were they shouting?'

'We were in their manor; they didn't like it. So we ran down the road, but they followed, running on the other side. Then a few of them got across the road when there was a gap in traffic, then they all began to cross over. We ran down a side street, trying to get away, but they followed. We ended up in some park, when they caught up with us.'

'That would have been London Fields.'

'If you say so. We all ran across the grass, then the others caught up with us. One of them had those... things: you know, two sticks chained together.'

'Nunchuks?' Jack asked. Nunchuks are a traditional Asian martial arts weapon comprising two sticks, traditionally wooden, connected to each other at one end by a short metal chain. They became part of Western culture and consciousness in the early 1970s, as a result of the popularity of Bruce Lee movies. In some countries, possession is illegal; in others it is designated as a regulated weapon. Under British law, they are not on the list of prohibited weapons, but public possession is heavily restricted. Therefore, it is unusual to see them in public.

'Yeah, those Kung Fu things. I think the guy who had them was Chinese, anyway.'

'So,' Jack asked, 'when you all reached the park, that's when the fighting started, is that right? Was Jaylon still with you?'

'I don't remember seeing him anywhere,' Derek replied. 'Everyone was running about. It wasn't long before we saw lots of blue lights and the police arrived. So we all ran different ways. I ran across the park and under a bridge. There's a station there, and I got on the first train that came, just to get away.'

'Leaving Jaylon there?'

'I told you, man; I didn't see him. He ran off somewhere. Look, I have to get back to work. You got my money?' He held out his hand.

'Here's your money,' said Jack, handing him a twenty and a ten, 'and here's my number. If you remember anything else, or you want to talk to me again, just call, okay?'

'Yeah, sure,' Derek said, pushing the money into his back pocket and turning back to the workshop.

'If I need to ask any more questions, I know where you are,' Jack called back. Derek did not respond.

Jack made his way back to his car, carefully avoiding the potholes on the access road. As he did so, he debated on whether he had learned anything that day, or whether it had been a waste of time. He quickened his pace as it began to rain.

CHAPTER NINE

JACK SAT IN his car, taking stock before pulling away.

What had he learned so far?

He had learned that Jaylon Soji was a quiet, retiring and solitary individual, who composed music and had the creativity needed to make outstanding model kits. He seemed to prefer his own company. He had no father figure in his life, and Jack had the suspicion that he was pampered by his mother. He also had the suspicion that he had to be persuaded to go out with his brother that fateful night.

But he was persuaded to remain with the gang

while his brother left, and to travel to Hackney with them. Not a million miles away, but it seemed out of character for him to have made the journey, without his brother, and with two strangers.

'My brother's a party pooper,' seemed very out of character for him to say. And then, when they arrived in Hackney, and were chased down the street by the rival gang, and into the park, when the fighting started, he apparently ran off. Not impossible of course, but something just didn't sit right.

He would need to talk to Jaylon himself. That was complicated by the fact that he was currently on remand in Pentonville Prison. He knew from a previous assignment the procedure involved in interviewing a prisoner, and this did not mean just showing up at the prison gates. He had never visited anybody at Pentonville before, but they would be following the standard Home Office procedure, and this meant that he would have to visit under the auspices of a member of his family. He could bluff, but it would be better to reach out to his mother to get her consent.

It was mid-afternoon now, so a prison visit would have to wait till the next day. He still had time to get over to Hackney and deal with things from the side of the victim. He would get over there now, and call Mrs Soji from home that evening; then he could book a visit online.

One fifty-minute drive later, and Jack had found a metered space outside the London Fields sports ground. He was on the west side of the park, and the block where Navindra Dhabi was killed, was across the park, on the east side. He walked across the park, looking about, trying to visualise the gangs fight that took place here that evening. That afternoon, it was quiet: the rain had given way to late afternoon sunshine. A single woman and a couple were walking their dogs, a man jogged past him, followed by a woman on a bicycle. He passed a bench where three youths were sitting, chatting and playing on their phones. They ignored him. As he got to the other side of the park, he was passed by three boys, early teens, in school uniform, also on their phones. It was that time of day again, he reflected: this time tomorrow, it would be Friday afternoon, and he would be meeting his own daughter as she finished school.

The road he reached was called London Fields East, and on the corner was a three floor block of flats called Blackstone House. This was the block where Navindra Dhabi lived, and where he died. The block of flats was one of those buildings where there was a long balcony, with five or six front doors positioned along it, each balcony joined by a staircase and maybe a lift, access to which was past a security door. He had no idea which flat the Dhabi family lived in; he had decided to go for the traditional approach and ask around, hoping that he would be sent to the right place.

Around the side of the building were two sets of doors, each up two steps. Jack knew which set of doors to head for as he could see flowers laid on the steps. They were remains of flowers, clearly been left for a while, probably just after the murder. All that remained were brown stalks, and dead heads lying, still wrapped up in dirty cellophane. Two of the three bunches had labels attached, but the writing on these labels had run in the rain and damp and was now illegible.

There was a stainless steel panel on the wall on which was printed FLATS 1-20, with twenty-one buttons below, two rows of ten, and a single one marked TRADES. There were no name labels, although to have one marked DHABI might have been asking too much. There was a small, rectangular window in the entrance door and Jack peered in. It was dark inside, but he could see it was a stairwell. He could make out the concrete steps leading up to the first floor, the first half dozen, at any rate. At the foot of the stairs, lying by the corner of the bottom step, were two more bunches of flowers; there was also a little votive candle, although not burning.

Jack looked around. On other occasions, where he was confronted with a door such as this, he would wait around until somebody else arrived, and follow them in, generally whilst pretending to be on a phone call. He, almost without exception, had learned that people never interrupted somebody else's mobile call. There was nobody around, and by loitering here, he ran the risk of looking suspicious. Even if he did get access, and he tried the door just in case, he had no idea which flat the victim lived in. He assumed numbers nineteen to thirty-six, but he could hardly go knocking on eighteen doors until he found the right one. Not at this stage, anyway.

He turned back to the park. The three youths were still congregating around the bench. He wondered if they knew the victim, or if he could get anything out of them. As he walked around the path, he could tell they were aware of him approaching, but did not acknowledge him, until he was about ten feet away, when one of them looked up from his phone at Jack.

'I'm sorry to bother you guys, but I wonder if you'd got a couple of minutes?' he asked. He passed a business card to the one who looked up, who appeared to be younger than then other two, and added, 'That's me. I'm here about the murder that happened over there.' He nodded over to Blackstone House.

One of the older ones was sitting on the bench armrest. He leant over and looked at the card Jack had given the younger man.

'You're a newspaper man?' he asked. 'A reporter?'

'I am. I'm trying to find out about what happened when that boy was murdered. Did any of you know him?'

'This for the newspaper?' asked the one who was standing up. He seemed older than the other two.

'Hopefully. If I can get enough copy.'

'What?'

'If I can get enough here to write about.'

'You gonna put our names in the paper if we tell you anything?'

'Only if you give your consent; otherwise it's all anonymous.'

The three looked at each other.

'So what you want to know?' the oldest asked.

'Did any of you know Navindra Dhabi, the boy who was killed?'

Everybody looked over at the older one, who replied, 'He was just some kid from around here. We didn't know him.' Jack shot a glance at the other two, looking for any signs of agreement or contradiction. Their faces were expressionless.

'O-kay,' he said slowly. 'What about the night he was killed: were any of you guys around? Did any of you see anything? Apparently there was a gang fight here that evening.'

The man shook his head and shrugged his shoulders. 'Sorry, mate. None of us was around then. We heard some shit had happened though. But we wasn't there.'

Again, the same blank expression on the others' faces: they just stared at the older guy, who seemed to be their spokesperson, then back at Jack.

Jack decided to try a different tack. 'All right. As I said, apparently there was a gang fight here that night. The fella who was arrested for the murder was from - with – a gang from further East – The Kings. Any of you heard of a local gang called the E8? You know, after the postcode? Any of you guys *in* the E8?'

'We don't know anything about no gangs,' the spokesman said. 'We can't help you, so why don't you fuck off and leave us alone?' He learned over and looked at the business card. 'Jack, is it? Why don't you hit the road, Jack, and never come back?' He started chanting a version of the Percy Mayfield song, laughing as he did so. The other two joined in.

'Fine. Sorry to be wasting your time.' Jack swung on his heels and walked back to his car.

CHAPTER TEN

IT WAS RAINING again when Jack arrived home, just after six. Even now, he was not sure how productive the day had been. Maybe a five out of ten; he had got some information, and he was hoping a visit to see Jaylon the next day would be a bigger step forward. He would call the boy's mother and get her consent, before going online and booking a visit.

As it turned out, she had no problem with Jack visiting. There were two forty-five minute slots, one at eleven o'clock and another at two thirty. She normally went at two thirty, but had another appointment the next afternoon, so was going to go at eleven. She consented to Jack visiting tomorrow afternoon, if that was going to help him get her son out of prison.

'Mrs Soji,' he cautioned, 'I just want to talk to him as part of putting together an article. I'm a reporter, not a lawyer.'

'I understand that, Mr Richardson, but every little helps, as they say.'

Poor woman, he thought as he ended the call: grasping at every straw. As any parent would in those circumstances. The call made, he lay on the sofa and messaged Cathy.

How you doing? Still on for the weekend?

Whilst waiting for her reply, he went online and booked his prison visit for the next afternoon.

Yes, I'll be there usual time came the reply.

I probably won't be in, I have an appointment at Pentonville in the afternoon.

The prison?

Yes

Dad, what have you been up to?

Very funny. Let yourself in. Have a look in the freezer and pick something for dinner. I think there's some lasagna or something in there.

Will do. What time do you think you'll be back?

Probably about 5. The appointment is 230, due to finish 315. Depends on the traffic.

Cool. I'll have your pipe and slippers ready.
Haha. See you tomorrow. Love you.
Love you too.

He leaned back and stretched. That was tomorrow sorted: now for tonight. He had a date. For a while now, he had been seeing a single mother named Susan Farmer. She, like Jack, was divorced, and had one child; her son, Kyle, was five or six years younger than Cathy. The relationship had been slow in developing, mainly because of their domestic circumstances. Jack was free Sunday to Thursday, not wanting to miss time with Cathy at the weekends; Susan was free mainly at weekends, as it was difficult for her to arrange childcare during the week. Kyle's father was out of the picture for all intents and purposes: Susan had said that he would probably refuse to have his son if it was to allow her to see another man. Now and again, she would arrange for Kyle to stay at her mother's so she could have an evening off. That was the case today: Grandma was meeting him from school, and Susan would pick him up from there the next morning, dropping him off at school on her way to work. These arrangements meant that Jack and Susan had to settle for daytime dates when they both took time off from work. They had both met and got on with each other's children, but their adult time was so difficult to arrange, so they would grab every opportunity.

Susan lived in the North London suburb of Cricklewood, not too far from Oakwood, where Jack's flat was. They had a table booked for eight PM at the Taj Mahal restaurant in Southgate, not too long a drive.

He had arranged to pick Susan up at her house at seven thirty, which would give them plenty of time to be arriving at eight, including time spent parking.

As it was, they arrived just after five past. The maître d' dismissed Jack's apologies for being late, and led them to a circular table for two, leaving them with a menu each. A waiter brought them a carafe of water and two glasses, returning five minutes later to take their order.

Jack ordered a Shami Kebab for a starter, and Susan, a Lamb Chatt. To follow, Jack chose a Cocktail Curry – chunks of lamb and chicken barbecued, blended with medium Mossala sauce, with grilled tomato, onion and capsicum. Susan ordered a Bakara Tikka – chicken prepared in a slightly hot curry sauce, served with a green chilli sauce, coriander, Indian herbs and yoghurt. They also ordered a bottle of the House White, although as Jack was driving, he would be sticking to the water after a couple of glasses.

The main course had just arrived when Jack's phone rang. He glanced at the screen: it was a number, but not one he recognised.

'I don't recognise the number, but I'd better see who it is, just in case,' he said apologetically.

Susan shook her head. 'Go for it.'

'Hello. Jack Richardson.'

'This is Levi.' There was a moment's silence, then, 'You gave me your card this afternoon. You said to call you if…'

'Yes,' Jack said. He stood up and mouthed to Susan that he had to take the call. She nodded. 'I'm sorry,' he said to Levi, as he walked out of the restaurant to take the call on the street. 'I wasn't expecting you to call, that's all.'

'You can talk?' Levi asked.

'Yes, sure. Thanks for calling me back.'

'I won't have long. I'm upstairs in my bedroom. Everyone else is out at the moment.'

'No problem. What did you want to tell me?'

'I couldn't say with the others there this afternoon, but I know who you were asking about.'

'The boy who was killed?'

'Yes.'

'The night he was killed: were you there?'

'I was. I knew him.'

'Well?'

'Eh?'

'How well did you know him? Are you both - were you both – in the E8 gang?'

'Both in the gang, yeah.'

'There was a fight between the E8 gang and a rival gang, The Kings. Was he involved with that? In the fight?'

'Everybody was, man. There was fighting everywhere.'

'Did you see Jaylon Soji?'

'Who's that, man?'

'He's the boy who was arrested for Navindra's murder.'

'I might have. Is he another Black guy?'

'He is. Black, tall – well over six foot. Bulky, though not fat.'

There was a pause.

'Yeah, might have done.'

'Who was he with, what was he doing?'

Another pause.

'Don't remember, man. There was a lot of shit going down that night. I just remember a dude like you described.'

'Did you notice him at all with the boy who died?'

'Don't know. Might have done.'

'They were probably heading over to that block of flats where they found Navindra's body. West of the park. Blackstone House, is it?'

'If you say so. I told you there was lots of shit going on. Then someone shouted out, "Police!" and there were blue lights flashing across the park, so I ran. I headed down in the direction of the canal, managed to get on a bus out of there.'

'And that's all you saw of him?'

'Look, man. I gotta go. That's all I can tell you.' With that, Levi hung up. Jack stared at his phone for a second, then pressed the red button to disconnect. He looked in at Susan: he had waved at her a couple of times whilst he was talking, just so she didn't feel she was being ignored. He put his phone back in his pocket and returned to their table.

'So sorry about that,' he said, sitting down again. 'Work call, obviously. I had to take it.' He gave her the gist of the story he was working on. 'He obviously couldn't talk to me with the others around: I was surprised he even called at all, so I had to take it, in case there was no other opportunity for him to call.'

'Was he on his own then?'

Jack nodded as he took a mouthful of warm food.

'In his bedroom, he said. Then he had to go.'

'Did he tell you much?'

Jack exhaled and wiped his mouth with his napkin.

'A little, I think. A pity nothing else.'

'He's got your number if he wants to talk to you again?'

'He does,' said Jack. He paused a second.

'And I have his.'

CHAPTER ELEVEN

'JACK – IT'S TIME to wake up. It's six thirty.'

Jack began to wake up to the sound of Susan whispering in his ear.

'You need to get up. I have to take a shower and go pick up Kyle,' she added.

Jack rubbed his eyes and looked at her. 'Already?'

'Yes. Look: I'll go downstairs and make coffee. You jump in the shower now.'

Jack grunted a yes, and stepped into the shower while she went downstairs. He was still in the shower when she returned five minutes later.

'Where do you want your coffee?' she asked

as she stepped into the bathroom. 'I'll put it down here.' She rested the cup on the side of the bath. 'I'll jump in when you're through.'

Jack reached out around the shower curtain. 'Think of the environment. Save water.'

'My tee shirt will get wet,' she said, adding, 'No, it won't,' as it slipped to the floor.

They stood in the shower, arms around each other. Jack leaned down to kiss her, and before long their tongues were entwined. Jack reached down and lifted Susan's right leg so it was curled around him; holding her tightly, he lifted her so she could wrap both legs around his waist. She put her arms around his neck, crying out as he entered her. It was not long before they both climaxed together, remaining frozen for almost a minute like two statues locked together in two places.

It was a ten-stop tube journey to Pentonville Prison. Jack's research had already shown him there was no public car park, and the surrounding roads were all permit parking only.

He got off at Caledonian Road station and walked down the same named road, two blocks to the prison.

It had been some years since Jack had been

here, and he was surprised to find that the walls were now whitewashed, at least the boundary wall and towers either side of the entrance driveway; also the front of the building, with its gothic architecture, triangular roof, and large, wooden arched doors. As he approached, he could see that the whitewashing was not extended to the other walls, only the front. The other walls were dark brickwork, with the large arched windows having their frames picked out in white. They looked freshly painted: maybe, he reflected, the Home Office budget only permitted the window frames to be repainted.

Once inside, the process was similar to what he had gone through when he had been to other prisons. He showed the e-confirmation on his phone, and got his QR code scanned. He used his driving licence for the required ID. He had to step through an airport-style gate, and had to endure a physical pat-down. Finally, he had to be checked out by a sniffer dog. Once through security, he was directed to the Visitors' Centre.

There were a dozen other people waiting in the centre. An officer came into the centre and ran through the visiting rules. One teenager was wearing a hoodie, and was told to take it off and leave it at the centre. Everyone had to leave their phones and other electronic devices in a safe deposit box here, a similar arrangement to when

Jack went to the Old Bailey the other day. The visitors had the chance now to purchase a token for refreshments which they could redeem at the tea bar. Jack was not in the mood for tea or coffee. The place depressed him, and he just wanted to talk to Jaylon and get out.

After the briefing had ended, Jack and the other visitors waited a few minutes; then another officer unlocked and opened a set of double doors with frosted panes, and indicated for the visitors to file through. They were taken down a corridor to a matching set of double doors, which were then opened. The doors opened into a hall in which were a number of tables – Jack counted twelve. Each table was at least six feet from the next, and had one seat one side, and two the other. Sat on the single chair, and dressed in blue denims and a grey sweatshirt was a prisoner. Some of the visitors started to gravitate towards a prisoner. Jack could see Jaylon sitting quietly at the back of the hall, his hands on the table. He looked bemused, and sad. Pathetic, in the literal sense of the word. There seemed a flash of recognition as Jack sat across the table from him.

'My name's Jack. Your mother gave me permission to come and talk to you.'

'I've seen you before,' said Jaylon. 'You were in the Court.'

'That's right.'

'I don't know you, though. My mother said you were from a newspaper.'

'That's right. I was sent to the Old Bailey to cover your trial for my newspaper. But you changed your plea to guilty, so there's not going to be a trial.'

'Oh, I see. They said something about getting reports. Then I suppose I'll be able to go home.'

Oh shit.

Somebody had to tell him he wasn't going home, but it wasn't going to be Jack. It had to be his mother. He made a mental note to call Mrs Soji as soon as he got out.

'Jaylon, tell me what happened.'

'What happened when?'

'That night over in Hackney. My understanding is that you went with your brother, out with his mates from the Kings gang. He wanted to go early, but you said you would stay longer with the boy called Derek and his cousin.'

'That's right. Jamal was being such a party pooper,' he sniggered. 'I wanted to stay longer as I was having fun with Derek. He said we were all going to go over to Hackney. So we did.'

'What happened when you got there? To Hackney, I mean. When you all got off the train.'

'Don't remember really. We walked down the High Street, then ended up in that park.'

'Did you go anywhere to eat?'

Jaylon looked at him blankly; then said, 'Yes, we did. KFC it was.'

'After you had your KFC, what happened?'

'Then some other boys started shouting across the road at us, so we ran off to get away from them. And we ended up at that park.'

'Where there was a lot of fighting,' Jack added.

'There was. It was a bit scary. I tried to run away.'

'Where did you run to?'

Jaylon frowned. 'I don't remember where. Just away.'

'Did you see or talk to the boy Navindra?'

Jaylon shook his head. 'Nobody.'

'You were found at the bottom of some stairs, inside one of the blocks of flats, next to Navindra's body. You were holding a knife. Do you remember that?'

Jaylon looked at Jack. He seemed puzzled.

'Think, Jaylon. Do you remember holding a knife?'

'I remember...' he said slowly. 'I remember holding a knife, yes.' As he spoke, he held out his right hand as if he was griping a knife. 'I remember lots of blood, all over my hands. I had to wipe them on my clothes to get the blood off.'

There was a moment's silence; Jack asked, 'Anything else? Do you remember anything else?'

'I remember the police coming. Blue lights flashing and stuff.'

Jack leaned forward slightly and spoke quietly.

'The boy Navindra. He was lying at the foot of the stairs. You remember all that blood: it was his. Did you kill him?'

'I must have done. The police told me I did.'

'Can you remember killing him? He was stabbed, and you were holding the knife.'

'I don't remember.'

'The knife: you said you remember the knife. Do you remember where you got it from?'

'That's a point,' Jaylon said. 'I remember holding the knife, but I can't remember where I got it from.'

'Did you bring it with you, or did anybody give it to you? Or did you just find it lying on the ground?'

'No, I don't remember how I got it, but I can remember holding it.'

Jack leaned back in his chair and took a deep breath.

'When you were arrested, you pleaded not guilty. Said you didn't kill him. Then, at the last minute, just as the trial was about to start, you changed your plea to guilty. Why did you do that?'

'Because I did it.'

'But you don't remember?'

'I must have done it. Everybody told me I did.'

'And that's why you changed your plea to guilty?'

'My solicitor told me to change it. He said my sentence would be better if I pleaded guilty, that I'd be able to go home sooner.'

'Okay,' said Jack, wearily. Out of the corner of his eye, he saw some of the other visitors getting up to leave. He decided he would do the same.

'Thanks for your time, Jaylon. Thanks for seeing me. All the best. I'll call your mother, let her know how things went.'

One of the officers indicated to Jack which way to go, back through the double doors, leaving Jaylon sitting alone at the table.

He left the prison as quickly as he could, and walked quickly back up to the station. He just wanted to get out of there and get home, and see his daughter.

CHAPTER TWELVE

YEARS AGO, WHEN Jack's marriage ended, the custody agreement in respect of their daughter Cathy set out that she would be based with Jack's ex-wife Mel, but that Jack would have access to her Friday afternoons to Sunday evenings. This meant in practice that he would pick her up from school Friday afternoon and return her home Sunday evening. This arrangement seemed to work well over the years, Jack's job allowing him to finish around two PM on Fridays.

For the last eighteen months or so, things had changed slightly as Cathy was old enough not to need picking up from school; in fact she considered this 'not cool'. She was able to make her own way home Monday to Thursday - a fifteen minute walk – and a bus ride of the same length to Jack's flat on Fridays. Logistically, this made things a bit easier for Jack, even more so once he had learned that she had a door key for home: he had provided her with a spare key for his place, and she was able to let herself in.

That is what happened this Friday: by the time Jack had got back from the prison, it was a quarter to five, and Cathy had let herself in, changed, made herself a drink and had got the lasagna out of the freezer, ready to cook.

'Hey, hey,' Jack said as he got in, kissing Cathy on the cheek and hanging up his coat. 'You got in then?'

'No sweat. And I got the dinner out. Were you in the office today?'

'No, I was up at Pentonville. I told you.'

'Yes, you did. I forgot. You were interviewing one of the prisoners.'

'Kind of. Some kid on remand.'

'What's he inside for?'

'Murder.'

'Wow. Who did he kill?'

'He's been charged with killing another kid, around the same age.'

'How?'

'You don't want to know.'

'Yes, I do.'

Jack sighed. 'Multiple stab wounds to the chest. And a slit throat.'

'God. And you're covering the trial?'

'There's not going to be a trial. He pleaded guilty.'

'So that's it? He just gets sentenced?'

'He's there pending pre-sentencing reports.'

'And you spoke to him to…?'

'To get his side of things. Get a balanced picture. I want to speak to the victim's family next week.'

'So you asked him how he did it? That was his confession?'

'He says he can't remember.'

'He can't remember stabbing someone multiple times?'

'Says not.'

'He did do it, didn't he? You said he pleaded guilty?'

'He didn't at first. That's why there was going to be a trial. Then, the morning the trial was about to start, it was announced that he had changed his plea to guilty. So the judge adjourned the trial.'

'Why did he change his plea at the last minute?'

'He said his solicitor advised him to. Solicitor or barrister, I'm not clear exactly who, but he was told if he pleaded guilty, his sentence would be lighter.'

'And that's true, is it?'

'Normally, yes; but something just doesn't feel right. He doesn't look or feel like a killer.'

'Oh dear.'

'What do you mean?'

'You're not just going to report on his trial, are you? You're going to try and prove him innocent.'

'I'm not sure yet. You don't have to prove innocence, by the way; you just have to refute the proof of guilt. Which hasn't gone before a court, before a jury.'

'Because he pleaded guilty?'

'Correct. So that's why I need to find out more about the victim. There is a gang connection, as well.'

'They were in gangs? Rival gangs?'

'The victim was. The kid I saw wasn't exactly. His brother is, but Jaylon -'

'Jaylon?'

'The name of the kid awaiting sentencing. He apparently just tagged along. His brother left early to see a girlfriend, and he stayed. He's not... not the sharpest tool in the shed, shall we say? What's that?' he added, pointing down at the kitchen top.

'That's garlic bread. I picked some up on the way back here. You have it with lasagna. I knew you wouldn't have any. Where did all this happen, by the way?'

'London Fields.'

'London Fields? Where's that? I've heard of it.'

'Hackney. East London.'

'Right,' Cathy said as she put the food in the oven.

'How's your mum, by the way?' asked Jack, hoping to change the subject.

'She's fine. You are still seeing Susan, aren't you?'

'Off and on. Saw her a couple of nights ago. Mum was asking, was she?'

Cathy grinned. 'You know Mum.'

'Is she still seeing that toyboy?'

'No, that ended a long time ago. No, it's just been her for a while.'

There was a moment's silence, then Jack asked, hoping to change the subject again, 'Looking forward to tomorrow?'

'The evening? Absolutely. A couple of girls in my class have seen it, and they say it's great.'

From then on, the conversation over dinner revolved around how Cathy was doing at school, how prepared she was for her next set of exams; a little of the conversation was around Jack's job: Cathy said her mother had commented that she had not seen Jack's name in the paper for a while, which made Jack wonder if Mel had actually read it as he had had quite a few pieces in there recently.

The conversation then moved to family, in particular Jack's sister Madeline. Madeline was widowed and had one daughter, who was away at university, and was, to use Jack's term, somewhat high maintenance. So much so that he avoided calling her, something for which he always felt guilty, but knew that their parents, who had retired to the South Coast, kept in regular contact with her, continually but in vain trying to get her to move out of South London and nearer to them.

'Have you spoken to your grandmother recently?' Jack asked, casually, whilst chewing some garlic bread.

'Which grandmother?' Cathy asked.

'Don't be evasive. You know which one I'm talking about.'

'She called me on my cell a few weeks ago. We chatted then.'

Jack nodded. 'Okay. She always asks after you when I speak with her. You know, there's no reason why you can't call her yourself now and again. You've got her number.'

'I will, I will.'

'Good. And what's all this "she called me on my cell"?'

Cathy held up her phone. 'On here.'

'Is that what you kids call them now? Your "cell"?'

'Oh,' she said, shaking her head, and putting the phone down. 'My mobile. Mum's taken to calling hers her cell phone. It's rubbed off on me.'

Jack laughed. 'So she's calling her mobile her cell phone? How long had she been doing that for?'

Cathy shrugged. 'Don't know. A while.'

'Why?'

She shrugged again. 'Don't know. Mum being Mum, I suppose.'

'Your mother being pretentious, I expect. Or watching too many American TV shows.'

'I suppose so.'

'More likely being pretentious,' Jack muttered, taking some more lasagna. 'So, any plans for the weekend? Apart from tomorrow evening.'

'Not especially. I thought I'd just chill tonight. I've got a shit load - sorry, shed load – of homework to do, so I'll do that in the morning. What time do we have to leave tomorrow?'

'It starts at seven thirty, so we need to aim to get there for seven. Factor in getting something to eat; I'd say leave here half two, three o'clock. There are plenty of places to eat in Victoria.'

'Cool. Looking forward.'

*****

They both cleared up and washed up, and Cathy announced she was going into her room to chill. She made herself a cup of tea and went into the room, closing the door behind her. Jack knew that meant she was going to watch something online or chat with her friends. He was not sure if that meant with school friends, those she hadn't seen for all of three hours, or others. He didn't know if that mean girl friends or boy friends. Boy friends, two words, or boyfriend, one word. This was one aspect of their daughter's upbringing which he and Mel had never discussed: perhaps it was time they did. He had considered raising the subject with Cathy herself, but decided against it: after all, if she had not felt she could tell him first, then there was no guarantee of getting an honest answer if he raised it with her himself. Best to talk to her mother first. He realised this was an area he knew nothing about. Then he had an idea: a couple of his work colleagues had children slightly older than Cathy; next time he was in the office maybe he could pick their brains.

As he settled down on the sofa with the TV remote, he could hear Cathy chatting in her room. It didn't sound like a girlfriend to boyfriend conversation: more like chatting with a classmate, as he picked up a couple of mentions of Mrs Somebody. Probably a teacher they were maligning.

Feeling relatively reassured, Jack began channel hopping. He got to Netflix, and ironically the menu screen was of latest movies, all eighteen-rated murder thrillers. Not something he found appealing tonight, as his thoughts kept returning to Jaylon Soji holding a bloodstained knife over the body of Navindra Dhabi.

He changed menu pages and came to comedies. Just what he needed. Somehow he got drawn to *Carry On Up the Khyber*, and settled for that.

But it was not long before he was asleep.

CHAPTER THIRTEEN

SATURDAY MORNING, AND Cathy was as good as her word. She made herself some toast and a cup of tea, and disappeared back into her bedroom. Jack looked in after he had showered and dressed. She was sitting on her made-up bed, laptop open, and the bed covered with various school books. She told him she should be finished by lunchtime.

He padded into his kitchen and made himself a cup of coffee, strong and black, and made some toast. At least she was doing her homework while under his supervision; if she hadn't, that would be another thing for her mother to give him earache about.

He logged on himself and checked the day's news, then checked that tube trains were running normally today. They were. While she was occupying herself with her homework, he was planning on drafting an outline for his article.

He went back into the kitchen to clear up, and notice the state of the cooker. It wasn't good. He was sure he had cleaned it last weekend - maybe the one before – but couldn't remember exactly. His normal routine was to clear the place up Thursday evenings in readiness for Cathy's arrival that afternoon, but Thursday he spent with Susan, evening and night. He grimaced, muttered, 'Shit,' then cleaned up the dishes and began to clean the cooker. He always tried to make sure his place was presentable for the weekend, especially the bathroom and kitchen, as it would only need one word from Cathy to Mel and there would be something else for his ex-wife to complain about. Of course, the place would get an extra once-over if he was expecting Susan to be staying over. It amazed him that her place was always so immaculate: how on earth did she find the time to keep on top of things?

Forty minutes later, he had finished in the kitchen and with the oven and moved to the bathroom. He really needed to be more prepared if he was expecting a guest, he thought, even if the guest was his daughter. That took fifteen minutes, after which he cleaned himself up, made yet another cup of coffee and returned to his notes and laptop.

As he sat down, Cathy came out of her room and went straight into the bathroom. On her way back, she paused in the doorway.

'Hey, how's the homework going?' Jack asked.

'Getting there,' she replied. 'Two more pieces to do. What about you?'

'Just about to start some prep on the piece I'm doing.'

'On that murder?'

'That's the one.'

'What time do we have to leave this afternoon?'

'Let's aim for two thirty. That will give us plenty of time to find a parking space at the station, get down there, and get something to eat.'

'Cool. I'll be done long before then.'

'See you later, then. Enjoy your homework. What subjects have you got?'

'I'm on History right now. Nearly done that; just Maths left. See you later.'

Cathy returned to her room and Jack turned back to his laptop, and the notes he had made the previous days. He checked through the information he had about London gangs, most of that gleaned from newspaper archives. He was not sure if he had enough information right now; maybe he needed some more, for padding if nothing else.

Ninety minutes later, he stopped, covered his face with both palms and rubbed his eyes. When he had typed 'gangs in london' into the search bar, he got 4,960 results, and he felt as if he had read them all, even though he had only scratched the surface. A lot of the articles related to people smuggling, an area he had had some experience with, mainly from Eastern Europe.

One article, which dated to December the previous year, had a reproduction of an Albanian advertisement on the TikTok site, featuring picture of the Christmas tree in Covent Garden. The advert promised asylum seekers trying to cross to the UK a special Christmas discount, namely £6000 for one person, £10,000 for two. They had to travel on December 20th. The standard price was £8000 per person. It seemed that traffickers were using social media more these days: when Jack was investigating a Russian gang of traffickers a few years back, everything was word of mouth. How times change, he reflected.

However, most of these pieces were concerned with people smuggling, and Jack was sure that was not the case here. The gang situation was more domestic, brought about in part by domestic situations. He narrowed his search.

One article, from a source he had never heard of caught his eye. It talked about gang members in London experience levels of post-traumatic stress disorder similar to troops in a war zone. Research had shown that living with violence, abuse in the home, and drug use all lead to this disorder. Again, Jack had assumed gang membership was a male bastion: apparently this was not the case: forty-five percent of gang members were females under the age of twenty-five. He glanced over in the direction of Cathy's bedroom, and shivered. The article went back to the subject of PTSD, and said there was a theory that a better understanding of the mental health of gang members could be crucial in tackling the capital's level of gun and knife crime, and sexual violence towards girls, who had become invisible victims.

Two words kept cropping up, and Jack felt these were more relevant than people smuggling.

County Lines.

That meant drugs.

He recalled that the whole purpose of The Kings going to Hackney that fateful evening was so that one of the gang members could carry out a financial transaction.

'Hmm,' Jack muttered, rubbing his chin.

*****

'You see?' Jack said as they sat on the Piccadilly Line train pulling out of Oakwood station. 'This is why you should always leave plenty of time for a journey.'

Cathy nodded, resignedly. 'Mum is the opposite.'

'So I recall. If she was coming, she'd still be in the shower now.'

Their journey to Victoria had not started well. They had left Jack's flat at just after two thirty; unexpectedly the car park at the station was full – two thirds full of cars, the other third by a giant puddle which was coned off. Much profanity later, Jack was able to find an on-street space three blocks away from the station. When they got to the station, they found there were severe delays owing to a broken down train at Bounds Green. Eventually they set off; then Jack learned from the TfL app that there were delays on the Victoria Line owing to an 'incident'.

'That means there's been a jumper somewhere,' he said as they pulled into Manor House. 'Forget changing at Finsbury Park; we'll go straight down to South Kensington, and hop on a Circle to Victoria.'

They eventually emerged into the late

afternoon sunlight at just before five.

'I know a nice place to eat not far from the theatre,' Jack said. 'I've not booked, but they should have a table for two at this time.'

The restaurant Jack had chosen was the Rail House Café, in Sir Simon Milton Square. At that time of the early evening they easily found a table for two. Jack ordered a minute sirloin steak, with a fried egg, and *salsa verde*, Cathy the buttermilk chicken in a bun, with pickled carrots, tomato and chipotle mayonnaise. Jack had a beer with his, Cathy a glass of mineral water. To follow, they both ordered sticky toffee brioche doughnuts, with a coffee.

Actually, Jack had chosen the restaurant deliberately as it was in the same building as the Victoria Palace Theatre, where they had two tickets to see the musical *Hamilton* at seven-thirty.

The show, written by Lin-Manuel Miranda and based on the biography by Ron Chernow, tells the story, in song and rap, of Alexander Hamilton, America's founding father. In two acts, it tells the story of Hamilton's life, including his part in the War of Independence as an assistant to George Washington, his marriage and career, and his relationship with Aaron Burr, which culminated in their duel, in which Hamilton was shot in the abdomen. He died the following day.

After the show, they headed directly back to Victoria station and the tube journey back home. They were both tired on the way home, and it was not long before Cathy dozed off, her head eventually resting on her father's shoulder. After they had settled down for the second leg of their journey, she fell asleep again, and Jack could feel his eyes closing. He fought it.

As the train clattered through the tunnel, through his half open eyes, he noticed the person sitting opposite. A youth, black, sitting alone, watching something on his phone. Jack's thoughts came back to Jaylon Soji. Earlier that day, he had uncovered a lot of information about the city's gang members and their life, with its constant undercurrent of violence. Their trip to the theatre had enabled him to temporarily put all that out of his mind, but now it was back to the real world. In spite of his intention to leave work until Monday morning, or Sunday evening at least, he began to figure out his next steps.

In the place of the youth sitting opposite, now he saw Jaylon Soji, alone, minding his own business on the train. Then he thought of Navindra Dhabi suffering a frenzied knife attack culminating in his throat being cut.

Somehow the two scenarios didn't quite fit.

CHAPTER FOURTEEN

THE WEEKEND OVER, Jack was in the office .

It was quite possible, logistically and technologically, for Jack to work exclusively remotely; however, the management of the *London Daily News* insisted that staff attend the office at least one day a week. 'So we can keep an eye on what you're all doing,' Mike Smith, the News Editor and Jack's supervisor, was wont to say, thinking he was being humorous.

Actually, Jack did not have a problem being in the office occasionally: it gave him a break from sitting alone in his flat, with just his laptop for company. Another reason was that if a major story was being allocated, he was of the view that it was more likely to be allocated to somebody who was physically in the office. Statistically, that probably was not the case, but it was a theory he clung to, rather than to admit he actually needed the company.

On his way into the offices on Silvertown Way in London's Docklands, he reflected on how quickly the weekend had gone. He was certain that if he had not had his daughter with him, it would have dragged. In his head, he calculated that it was sixty-five hours since he had got home to find her already there, cooking the dinner. A far cry from only a few short years back when he had to rush home every Friday afternoon, to pick up the car, to drive over to her school for three PM. If he was honest, he was not sure which he preferred: having even more time to himself now she was more independent and able to do things and travel on her own, or when she needed him to pick her up from the school. In some small way, he missed the rush to get to the school at three. maybe if he and Mel had stayed together longer, Cathy might have had a younger sibling and he would still have to hurry to the school. But that was just fanciful thinking.

He walked straight into the office, past the now permanently unoccupied reception desk, and headed to his own workstation. There was a flat screen monitor and keyboard, which he pushed aside to make way for his own laptop. He had planned on doing more research on gangs over the weekend, after he had dropped Cathy off at her mother's, but spent the evening surfing, checking and answering emails. They had both slept in late Sunday morning, decided to forgo brunch as they were both still full from the previous evening, went for a walk at lunchtime, then took the car back to Mel's. He generally had some kind of conversation with his ex-wife: sometimes it was a brief chat on her doorstep; other times he was invited in for a coffee or a drink. It was the former yesterday, so it was a brief 'See you Friday' to Cathy and 'See you next Sunday' to Mel.

The office was quiet that morning. He could see that Mike Smith was in his office; or rather, could hear he was in his office, as he was talking very loudly on his mobile. He was one of those people who felt that if the person to whom he was on the phone was some distance away, he needed to talk loudly, so they could hear him. Unfortunately, so did the entire office. Only two other colleagues were in: Cliff Hughes, the Entertainment Correspondent, and Eddie Hutchinson, the Sports Writer. Jack tried to shut out the sound of Mike's voice as Eddie approached.

'Hey, Jack; how's it going?'

Jack leaned back in his chair and crossed his arms. 'Slow going, to be honest, mate.'

'Why? What are you working on?'

Jack gave his workmate a potted version of his story so far.

Eddie nodded. 'Gangs,' he muttered. 'Are people that interested in all that shit? I mean, how many gang-related stories have we run over the years?'

'It's trying to get something out of the murder trial I was supposed to be covering.'

'Trial? Where? The Bailey?'

'It was. Then he pleaded guilty, so that was it. I'm just trying to squeeze something out of what is really a non-story. What are you working on?'

'Well,' Eddie chuckled. He looked round and pulled up a chair at the side of Jack's desk. 'Have you heard of Sonny Lincoln?'

'The football player? Of course I have. What's he been up to?'

'He and his wife have split up. Probably an acrimonious divorce battle coming up, which I'm looking forward to covering. But…' He leaned forward to talk to Jack *sotto voce*, even though the nearest person was fifty feet away. 'I interviewed the fragrant Mrs Lincoln over the weekend, and it seems the illustrious star player had some shall we say deviant sexual appetites.'

'Like what?' Jack asked, himself looking round to make sure they were not being overheard.

'For a start,' Eddie began, 'he liked his sex rough. And I mean *rough*. And he was rather partial to escort girls.'

'A top division football star into escort girls? Eddie, that's some newsflash.'

'I know, I know, but this is the *piece de resistance*.' His voice was now little more than a whisper. 'Have you ever heard of iglooing?'

Jack looked at him with a blank expression. 'That's what eskimos do?'

Eddie shook his head. 'It's where you take a crap. You put it in a condom *somehow*, then put said condom in the freezer. Then when it's frozen, you use it as a dildo. On yourself.'

'No shit?' said Jack. 'Sorry, mate; couldn't resist that. And Mrs Lincoln knew nothing of this?'

'Absolutely nothing. They apparently have two freezers: one in the kitchen and one in an outbuilding. She had cause to get something out of the second freezer one evening, and between the frozen peas and vanilla ice cream, what should she find, but -'

'I get the picture,' Jack said. 'So that's going to feature in a piece? That Sonny Lincoln is a scatophiliac?'

'What the hell's that? Scato...?'

'It's what you just told me. Is there anything else he -'

He was interrupted by Mike Smith arriving on the scene.

'Jack, how are things? You got time to give me an update? Save you having to type an email.' He walked back to his office. Jack raised his eyes to the ceiling to Eddie and followed Mike. He sat down the other side of his supervisor's desk, and brought Mike up to speed.

'So,' Mike said once Jack had finished, 'you haven't got very much.'

'Not at the moment,' Jack conceded.

'I was hoping for a nice juicy murder trial. Especially considering how the victim was killed. But there's no trial now; only a sentence.'

'You said to expand things to talk about gang violence.'

'Yeah, I did. But I've had second thoughts about that. Maybe gangs have been done to death, if you pardon the expression. What do you think?'

'I think he doesn't look like a murderer. The way the other kid was killed, it looks like the return of Jack the Ripper.'

With a weary tone, Mike said, 'And you're saying he didn't do it?'

'That's the opinion I'm forming.'

'I don't want you going off on one of your wild goose chases.'

Jack said nothing.

After a few seconds, Mike said, 'Look, it's Monday, late morning. You've got until we go to press Wednesday night. Then, you'll have to start another story. You might need to do that anyway. Alf Coleman's gone down with the flu or something, so you might need to take over what he was working on.

'You've got just over forty-eight hours.'

CHAPTER FIFTEEN

'YOU COMING OUT for a beer, Jack?'

Jack looked up at his colleague Cliff Hughes, who was leaning over the partition adjacent to his desk. He knew Cliff was partial to a lunchtime drink – he was, in a way, a remnant from the classic Fleet Street era of newspapermen – and it smelt as if he had already started.

Jack checked the time on his phone. It was eleven forty-five. He was surprised the morning had gone so quickly.

'Some other time, mate? I've got quite a lot on today.'

Cliff sniffed and pushed himself off the

partition. 'Suit yourself. I'm having one.'

'Only one?' Jack chuckled to himself as he watched his colleague head for the door. Much as he would have enjoyed a pint or two, it was not to be: he was being truthful when he said he had a lot on. He now had forty-eight hours - forty-six now, to be precise – to move this story forward before it was killed. In theory, if he was assigned something else, he could carry on with this, but in his own time; however, he had tried that before, and it did not work very well.

So, to all intents and purposes, he had until the day after tomorrow. Wednesday evening.

He had already made some progress. He wanted to get some background information on the victim. This would mean a return to the block of flats where the murder took place, and knocking on every door in the block if he had to. He also needed to speak with Jaylon's legal representation, but he needed to have the consent from his mother. To that end, he called Mrs Soji immediately after he was given his deadline, and explained what he needed and why he needed it.

'Well, if you think it will help Jaylon,' she had said.

'It definitely will, Mrs Soji,' he assured her. *It couldn't do any harm* was probably a more accurate phrase.

'Then please speak to him.'

'The thing is, though, is that he or she will need your consent before they will talk to me. Could I ask you to call them and give them that consent?'

'I can do that if it will help,' she repeated.

'Thank you very much. And you'll let me know when you have done so? Then I can call them. Who are the solicitors, by the way?'

'It's a Mr Edge, from Gupta and Edge. In Romford.'

'Fine. Call me back once you have spoken to Mr Edge.'

'I will, Mr Richardson. I'll call you straight back.'

She was as good as her word, although what she said was not quite what Jack had in mind.

'I've spoken to him, Mr Richardson, and he says he can see you this afternoon at a quarter past three.'

A trip to Romford was not what he had in mind, particularly as he had left his car at home, but he had little choice.

'Okay, fine. Thanks for arranging that. I'll see Mr Edge this afternoon.'

The offices of Gupta and Edge were in North Street, just off the Market. Jack's journey planner told him it would take fifty-eight minutes from his desk to the offices, so he planned on leaving by one-thirty, his planner being notorious for underestimating journey times.

Saying nothing to any of his colleagues, he left at half past one. He noticed that Cliff Hughes had still not returned to his desk, but he thought he could make out his colleague's figure in the distance as he got out into the street, so he walked briskly up the road to avoid bumping into him.

Romford Market Place is a mere five minutes' walk from the station. His journey suffered no delays, and so he arrived with twenty minutes to spare. The market was not open that day – Jack had no idea of the days it was held – and the whole space seemed eerily deserted that afternoon. He bought himself a latte and sat in the Costas branch on the corner until ten past, when he walked across the street to the offices.

A tarnished silver plate on the wall was embossed with GUPTA AND EDGE CRIMINAL DEFENCE SOLICITORS, and was adjacent to a wooden door, dark blue, but in need of a repaint. Jack climbed the stairs to the first floor, went through a glass door with the same endorsement, and into a small office. A tiny Indian lady sat behind a desk, the PC screen almost concealing her.

He was obviously expected. 'Mr Richardson?' she asked. Jack nodded and was shown into one of the two offices, with a door marked JULIAN EDGE.

Edge was standing by his desk as the lady showed him in. The office was small, untidy, and strangely smelt of cigarette smoke, which surprised Jack, as smoking had been illegal in the workplace for some years. Unless the smell came from Edge himself, which, as he approached, Jack realised it was.

Edge asked Jack to sit down and did so across the desk. He was a tall, wiry man, mid-fifties, fair hair with a receding hairline. At first, Jack though he was stooping, then then through he was round shouldered, then came to realised that he had a small hump at the top of his back. As Jack sat down, he had a feeling of sympathy: for Edge himself, and for Mrs Soji, who had to engage Edge, whose fees were surely at the lower end of the spectrum.

Edge spoke first.

'So, Jaylon Soji. His mother called me and gave her consent so I can discuss this with you.'

'Yes, that's right.'

'Nice boy.'

Jack asked, 'Do you think he did it?'

'I don't really care,' Edge replied evasively. 'I'm paid to represent him.'

'I've been to see him at the prison. He told me you advised him to change his plea to guilty.'

'Look – you've seen the evidence?'

'Not exactly, but I'm familiar with the facts of

the case.'

Edge took a deep breath, and sat back in his chair. 'He was found at the other boy's body, covered in the boy's blood. He was holding the knife that killed the boy. The victim was still warm – very warm.'

'Having only just died?'

'Within minutes according to the pathologist. There was nobody else around. There were traces of the victim's DNA on Jaylon's clothing, suggesting some form of struggle; you know, the victim trying to defend himself. Seems an open and shut case.'

'So how can you defend something like that?'

Edge sighed again. 'He's been saying he can't remember anything. Sadly, under English law, amnesia is not a defence. If you've met him, you would have noticed… how can I phrase this tactfully and professionally? He's not very bright. I don't know whether he'd actually be classed as special needs, but something's not right with him.'

'Does he understand what's going on?'

'I'm not sure, to be honest. His mother and brother certainly do, and he talks to both of them a lot. Seems to hold what his brother tells him in high regard.'

'So why, if the evidence is so overwhelming, did he plead not guilty to begin with? And why change it to guilty just before the trial?'

'He pleaded not guilty at the beginning because his brother told him to, not to put too fine a point on it. It was my view and that of the barrister we engaged, that he should had pled guilty, and we would use a defence of diminished responsibility. But he was being cajoled by his mother and brother and insisted on a not guilty plea. But we were finally – at the last minute, as you say – able to convince him to change his plea. An argument we used was that if we used the defence of diminished responsibility and avoided the expense of a trial, then his sentence would be lighter, once the Court has evaluated him and his condition. That seemed to be the catalyst for his change of heart.'

Edge paused and looked Jack in the eye.

'Any more questions, Mr Richardson?'

CHAPTER SIXTEEN

Jack eschewed public transport the following day, and drove down to London Fields. The time in the car gave him the opportunity to reflect on how things had gone the previous day. He had travelled back home from Romford during the rush hour, and with moving around to give people who were alighting access to the doors and squeezing himself in amongst London's unwashed, all he wanted to do was get home, shower, eat and chill.

Speaking to Jaylon's solicitor was something he had to do, but he was still not sure what he had got out of the conversation. He already knew

Jaylon was a nice guy; he already knew it was an open and shut case, but there was still that feeling he had had in the courtroom and when he went to the prison. Perhaps that was all it was: just a feeling, without any logic or facts. Everything that Julian Edge had said yesterday made sense. Maybe Mike Smith was right, and there was no story here, and Jack was wasting his time.

'Forget it,' he said aloud. He was driving east on the North Circular, about to approach the Great Cambridge Junction, where he would turn right onto the Great Cambridge Road, which would take him down to Hackney. All he had to do was make a one eighty on the roundabout, and head back the way he came. He was now on the slip road, the exit leading to the roundabout. It went up a hill, the North Circular continuing through an underpass. He had already moved into the right hand lane, and began to circumnavigate the roundabout. He was still in the lane to head down the A10 Great Cambridge Road, and needed to filter to the right to get in the right lane for his one-eighty. However, while he was considering what to do, the lane to his right was now filled with two HGVs, effectively blocking him from filtering right; he had no choice now but to join the A10.

'Shit,' he muttered, feverishly thinking about where he could turn round, although that might difficult as this was a very busy stretch of road. 'Oh, what the hell,' he finally said. It looked as if fate had decided he should go to Hackney that morning.

He continued with the slow journey on this road, turning off at Dalston Junction, and threading his way through the narrow residential streets. The next challenge would be to find a parking space.

Driving along one street, he noticed a car pull away a couple of hundred yards further up. He was driving at around twenty at this time, a light touch on the accelerator raised the speed by five miles per hour. Almost at the space, he realised he had no need to speed up as he was driving along a one-way street; however, he soon reached the recently vacated space and pulled in. In the old days, there would have been a coin-fed meter here: now there was a sign with a QR code for Jack to scan and pay for his parking that way.

He had parked a seven minute walk from the block of flats he was headed for: there may have been closer spaces, but he had no desire to waste time driving around looking for spaces if there was nothing closer. He had bought three hours parking, which should be more than enough.

He reached the block of flats, and headed directly for the door he went to the other day. Peering through the little window, he saw the flowers were still at the foot of the steps, although they, too, were almost dead.

To talk to anybody here he would need to get inside: his tried and trusted method was to wait around at a discrete distance until somebody arrived; then pretend to be making a call while following the person in. Invariably, they would hold the door open for him or allow him to hold the door for them. In all the years of doing this, he had never been challenged, giving verisimilitude to the idea that nobody ever interrupted a mobile phone conversation.

This time, however, he might not have to wait. He noticed, at the bottom of the panel of doorbells, the button marked TRADES. He pressed it, waiting to see what happened. Immediately, he heard a click as the door was unlocked. Without delay, he opened the door and stepped inside, astonished it was as easy as that.

Experience had taught him that in situations such as this, it was better to be upfront and put his cards on the table, show his business card, say who he was and what he was looking for.

This part of the block contained forty flats, ten on each of the four floors. He took a deep breath and started at Number 1.

No answer.

He knocked at Number 2.

No answer.

Number 3.

No answer.

He sighed. A lot of his work was tedious: waiting for things or people. Knocking at doors. He walked down the corridor to Number 4 and knocked there.

He could hear a TV playing, so he assumed somebody was in. After a few moments, the door opened, and a grey-haired woman stood in the doorway.

'Can I help you?' she asked. She spoke with an accent which Jack took to be somewhere African.

Jack gave the woman a business card by way of introduction, and explained why he had called.

'I read about all that in the paper,' she said.

'Yes, this is for a background piece.'

'That's what all those flowers over there are about, isn't it?' she said, looking down the corridor.

'I assume so, yes.'

'I'm sorry, I can't tell you much. I was in when they said it happened, but I didn't hear anything. The door was bolted and the TV was on. Then I read it in the paper a few days later and thought, "My God, that's here!"'

'Do you know the family, or which flat they're in?'

'No, I'm sorry; I don't.' She paused a second. 'But I know who might be able to.'

'Yes?' said Jack, praying for a breakthrough.

'You could try Mrs Hawtrey upstairs. Flat 16, I think. She never goes anywhere; knows anything about anyone. Everything about everyone, I should say. Try her.'

'Mrs Hawtrey. Flat 16,' Jack repeated to confirm. 'I'll try her. Thanks very much.'

After she had closed her door, Jack glanced down the corridor. He considered knocking at the other six doors, then decided he would try short-circuiting the whole process and knocking at Flat 16. That could save him a lot of time.

He climbed up to the next floor, carefully stepping over the flowers at the foot of the steps. His foot hovered over the bottom step as he looked down at the almost dead flowers. There were three separate bunches lying there, one totally dead, the other two almost. The almost dead bunches had cards attached but these had been wet and were crumpled. The writing on the top card had run and was now illegible. It might have been the smell of the decomposing flowers, but Jack caught a faint whiff of urine as he climbed the concrete steps.

He rang the doorbell at Number 16. He could hear voices inside, and momentarily a man opened the door. He was elderly, short with a bald head, white hair around the edges. He was wearing a vest and shabby grey tracksuit bottoms.

'Yes?' he asked.

'Er, I was looking for Mrs Hawtrey,' Jack enquired. Through the doorway he could see a woman on one of the balconies the other side of the building. She was hanging out washing.

'Esme!' the man called out. She came indoors and walked to the door.

'The man wants to talk to you,' Mr Hawtrey said, and went back indoors.

'Can I help you?' Mrs Hawtrey asked.

Jack introduced himself again, adding, 'The lady at Number 4 said you might be able to help me.'

'Did she now?' Mrs Hawtrey said, reading Jack's card. 'You're asking about the Dhabis upstairs. Number 25, aren't you? Is this for your newspaper?'

'It is, yes; just some background information, if you can.'

'Will I get a mention in your paper?'

Jack found sometimes it paid to appeal to people's vanity. 'Yes, unless you want to remain anonymous.'

'What about a photograph?'

He groaned inwardly. 'That will be up to my editor. You know the family?'

'I know them. They're away at the moment. Left just after the boy was killed.'

'How many in the family?'

'The father, the mother, and two brothers. Plus the dead one. His brothers are twins, younger than him.'

'Okay.'

She shook her head and pulled a face as if confronted by a bad smell.

'I never liked them. Him. The dead one.'

'Really? Why not?'

'He was always hanging around the place with some other kids. On the stairs, by the door. Out in the park. Always sniffing around the girls that live around here.'

'In what way?' Jack asked.

'He and the other kids. Around the same age, some a bit older. Stopping the girls and asking if they had any cash. My granddaughter was visiting in the summer and my husband had to walk her across the park to the bus stop. I think they're on drugs.'

'Oh? What makes you say that?'

'You can see them sitting on one of them benches out in the park, smoking something. You see that playground at the corner of the park? With the swings and slides? I was there one day in the summer with my grandson watching him on the slide and they came over, standing behind me. Not right behind me; the other side of the railings. But I felt so uncomfortable I had to bring him indoors. Shouldn't be allowed. And the smell of what they're smoking…'

'The smell?'

'Sort of sweet, sickly.'

'They could be vaping. You can get different flavours.'

'I don't know about all that. My husband calls it wacky baccy.'

'Have the police ever been called?'

'Now and again. There's quite a bit of crime that goes on around here; mostly the kids. You see police cars now and again. Mainly at night, the blue lights, you know? We had a murder here a few years ago - another murder. A woman in one of the other blocks got beaten to death. My husband said she was on the game. I don't know if they ever caught whoever did it.'

'The other kids he hung around with: do you know any of them?'

'Nah. All from around here, I suppose. Nobody goes very far here.'

'Do you know where the family have gone, or how long they're away for?'

'No idea, sorry. All I know is, they disappeared a day or so after the murder. You might try 24 or 26: they might know more than me.'

'I will. Thank you very much for your time.'

'You're welcome, love. I'm Mrs Hawtrey. Will you be sending a photographer down then?'

CHAPTER SEVENTEEN

JACK CLIMBED THE stairs to the second floor. He was headed to doors 24 and 26. He thought he might as well knock on all the doors while he was on this floor: it couldn't hurt, and they might have more information living on the same floor. He sighed and knocked on the first door: number 20.

He waited a few seconds after knocking before trying a second time. There was no doorbell. He could hear the muffled thump of music playing, maybe a voice on the soundtrack: it was difficult to tell if it was coming from this flat or one of the others. He was sure the walls in this place were paper-thin, anyway.

He was about to put an ear to the door when he heard a noise from the end of the corridor. A woman was leaving the flat with a shopping trolley. As she approached Jack, she said, 'I wouldn't waste your time there, dear; they're both out at work all day.'

'Not to worry,' said Jack. 'I'll put a note through their door. Actually,' he added as he fished a business card out of his pocket, 'this is me here. I'm covering a piece around Navindra Dhabi's killing. I'm aware that the family is away, but I was asking the neighbours if they could tell me anything about Navindra himself. Sort of human interest angle.'

She studied his card for a second, muttering, '*The News.*' She looked up at him. 'Well, I can tell you a bit, not much. I didn't - don't, I should say – know the family that well. Only just to say hello to, passing on the stairs, that sort of thing, you know?'

'What about Navindra himself? The boy who died?'

She pulled a face and shook her head a little. 'Well, you don't like to speak ill of the dead, do you?'

Jack tried to coax more out of her. 'But…?'

'I'll be honest with you: I didn't really like him. I know he's not with us anymore, but you have to tell the truth, don't you?'

'Why didn't you like him?'

'There was something about him. Not because he was… whatever he was, Asian or something. I'm not racist. But there was something about him. He always had that look on his face.'

'What type of look?'

'It was as if he knew something about you. As if he was secretly laughing at you. Something like that. His mother and father seemed very pleasant, the odd times I saw them, their other two children, too. But him…'

'Some of the other neighbours said he was always hanging around with other young men,' Jack exaggerated.

'Oh my God, don't get me on that. Always there, like a bad smell. At the bottom of the stairs or in the doorway or one of those benches out in the park. All hours too; he couldn't have had a job. Why his mother and father didn't…. Oh, well; that's all in the past now, I suppose.'

'Were you around the night he was murdered?'

'Yes, I was, but I didn't see anything. It was late, it was dark, and I had the curtains drawn, and the television on. I think I could hear some commotion outside on the Green, but didn't even bother to look out. As long as they stay outside, I keep myself to myself. But, that night, I had to go into the kitchen, and that meant walking past the spare bedroom. The curtains weren't drawn, and through the nets, I could see two, maybe three, blue lights. So I thought police, ambulance, you know? I had a quick look through the nets and could see, I think it was three police cars and an ambulance. Then I thought I could hear a lot of talking from downstairs, so I went outside, in the passage out there, and I could tell the talking was happening in this block. I walked down to the stairs and had a look over the landing. I couldn't see anything, and I couldn't quite tell what they were saying. Mrs Madell from number 28 came out as well. We listened for a bit, then went back indoors.'

'And you saw nothing else?'

'I checked a few times later in the evening. The blue lights were still there, although I think the ambulance had gone. They were still there when I went to bed. When I got up the next morning, everything had gone as if nothing had happened.'

Jack nodded. 'Well, thanks for your time.' He pointed to the business card she was holding. 'My number's on there. Give me a call if you think of anything else. What flat number are you? Just so I don't knock there unnecessarily.'

'I'm flat 28.' She picked up her little shopping trolley and began to carry it down the stairs.

'Would you like a hand with that?' Jack asked.

'It's all right, thank you. I do this every day.'

'You could do with a lift here.'

'We certainly could. Goodbye, then.'

Jack turned and resumed knocking on doors. The next door, number 21, was the source of the loud music. This time there was a doorbell: he rang that and within a minute the door was answered by a man. Black, grey curly hair, middle-aged. He was wearing a tee shirt in the colours of the South African flag and the logo INVICTUS GAMES printed on the front. Jack handed him a card and introduced himself.

The man looked at the card, shook his head and gave the card back to Jack.

'Nothing to say, mate. Why don't you people leave them alone?'

'I was just looking for…'

'Nothing to say.' With that, the door was closed in Jack's face.

'Oh, well; you can't win 'em all,' Jack muttered to the closed door, then stepped to the next. No answer, so he wrote a short note on a card and posted it through the letter box.

It was the same with the next door. And the next.

Now he came to the Dhabi flat. He tried ringing the doorbell. He could hear the bell ringing inside, but that was it. Making sure the corridor was clear, he crouched down and looked through the letterbox. Inside, the place seemed still furnished, but silent. He stood up. Nothing surprising there. It was not surprising that nobody was in. The neighbour had told him the family had gone away, which would have been understandable in the circumstances. It looked, though, that they were planning on coming back. Or were they? They may have rented the flat fully furnished.

The smell of cigarette smoke hit Jack as soon as the door of number 27 opened. Jack put the age of the girl who opened it as late teens, early twenties. She was smoking a cigarette, wore a tight vest which left no contour of her body hidden and the briefest of miniskirts. Her hair was cropped to the neck and was the colour of straw on the left hand side and a shade of purple the other. She had two rings through her left ear, one through her right nostril and one through her lip. As she spoke, Jack could see a stud in her tongue. His first thought was how does she cope with airport metal detectors.

'Yeah?' she mumbled.

Jack went through the usual routine of handing out a business card and explaining who he was and why he was calling.

She looked at him blankly before saying, 'Is that that kid next door?'

'Yes, did you know him?' Jack nodded.

She shrugged. 'Not really.'

'Did you see him around? Apparently he used to hang around downstairs and on the Green. With some other guys,' he added, hoping that would prompt more information from her.

'Nah,' came the reply.

'Did you ever see him around?' Jack pressed. 'The boy Navindra?'

'Might have done, now and again. Didn't talk to him, though.'

'Would your... parents know anything?' Jack asked tentatively.

'My mum left us years ago and my old man's at work all the time. Only me and my brother most of the time, ok?'

'Would your brother know anything?'

'I don't know; he's at school.'

Jack nodded. 'I see. Okay. Would he have known Navindra?'

'Unlikely. He's four.'

'I see,' Jack said. 'Look, keep my card and if anything comes to mind, give me a call on that number.'

She read the card again. 'Will we get in the paper if we do?'

Jack sighed inwardly. 'Maybe,' he nodded. He turned and left, and the girl shut the door. There was no answer the other side of the Dhabi flat, so yet again, he out a card and note through the letter box and left. Once outside, he pulled his coat collar up around his neck as he was hit by a cold wind. He looked back up at the block of flats, and felt he had done enough here for the day. Time to drive back home and put together all he had picked up today.

He walked back to where he had left his car. Almost at the car, he heard a voice: thinking nothing of it, he pressed the unlock switch on his key fob and the indicator lights flashed.

Then the voice again. 'Hey, I'm talking to you.'

He stopped by his car and turned around. Walking down the street towards him were two men. They looked strangely familiar, then Jack realised where he had seen them before. They were two of the three males he spoke to the other day. They were sitting on one of the park benches then. The third – the one who called – was not there. What was his name? Jack remembered: Levi.

'Yes?' Jack asked, suspicion in his voice. His eyes darted around: apart from the parked cars, the street was empty.

'You're asking a lot of questions,' the older male said.

'It's my job,' Jack asked.

They stared at him for a second, not understanding his answer.

'I work for a newspaper,' Jack explained.

'You ain't talking to no one, motherfucker,' the older male spat, pulling out a knife.

CHAPTER EIGHTEEN

JACK LOOKED DOWN at the knife.

The second his brain registered *knife,* he envisaged a combat knife or a fighting knife, a Bowie, maybe; but in reality it was a domestic kitchen knife. Six inches long, maybe, without a serrated edge. He felt a sense of relief that this was all it was, but it could still do a lot of damage. It looked sharp.

The fact it was a domestic knife reassured him a little as to the type of people he was dealing with. Not professionals; more likely some idiot who had grabbed a knife out of the kitchen drawer before he left home. Jack had no idea how he was able to carry the knife around, concealed.

He was not prepared to take any chances, though. At least he was bigger than they were, although he was not sure if his greater size and strength were enough to take on both of them at the same time. He already had his hand on the car door: in the same movement, he opened the door, positioning himself partially behind it, and turned to the men. 'What are you talking about?' he asked, irritably.

Now, the car door was open, and hung between Jack's right leg and the knife holder's left leg. In the space of two seconds, he shuffled half a step back, raised his right leg enough to put his foot on the car door, and pushed forward hard. The door swung back, the edge catching the left knee of the knifeman, who cried out in pain as he bent over, clutching his injured knee with both hands. As he did so, the knife clattered onto the kerb. Jack grabbed the door handle again, pulled the door open, and slammed it back hard onto the man, catching him on the head and shoulder. He was now on all fours.

Jack had both hands on the car door, about to pull the door back to deliver a second blow, when the second one leapt at him. No weapon, just bare hands. Jack was aware of the knifeman lying on the pavement, groaning and nursing his knee, but could not see where the knife landed. He needed to kick it out of reach, under the car or something. As his eyes darted to the ground, his collars were grabbed by the second guy. Their faces were six inches apart, and Jack could smell his attacker's breath: a rancid mixture of stale spicy food and God knows what.

At the front of the head, the skull is around fifteen millimetres thick; the bone at the ridge of the nose is around three millimetres. The moment Jack's forehead made contact with his attacker's face, he could feel the other man's nose give way. With a cry, the other man staggered back, clutching his face, which was already bleeding profusely, blood seeping through his fingers. Jack could feel a wetness on the front of his head, which he knew was not his own blood.

Clutching his face with both hands, the man staggered back, as if expecting another blow from Jack, then turned and ran up the street awkwardly.

It was then that Jack realised he had miscalculated. Or taken his eyes off the ball. Or maybe the odds were against him.

One man against two.

Two plus a knife.

Jack cried out in pain as, still on the pavement, the first attacker plunged the kitchen knife into his upper leg. Still reeling from the shock and pain he swivelled and, with his left leg and holding onto the car door for support, kicked out at the man, catching him in the stomach.

That was enough, for both the man who struggled to his feet and ran up the street in the same direction as his associate. Enough, too, for Jack, who had to lean against the car to catch his breath. He looked down at his leg. Around three inches of the blade were protruding: that was good, he thought, as it meant that no more than three inches was imbedded in his leg. Also, there was less blood than he would have thought: maybe he had been lucky as to where the blade had gone in. That might change, of course, when he pulled he knife out.

He propelled himself to the car boot, and rummaged through the contents. He found a couple of plastic supermarket bags. *Bags for Life* they were called: ironic, he thought. He tore the bags into strips and tied them tightly around the top of his leg, just above where the knife was protruding.

He needed to get to a hospital, preferably one near home. His nearest one was Barnet Hospital, but it would not have been a good idea to drive. He went online on his phone and found that the nearest hospital with Accident and Emergency facilities was Homerton University Hospital. That had to be no more than ten minutes' drive from there.

He recalled what he had read before about stab wounds, namely that he should not remove the knife, as it may be acting as a plug, which could explain why there was not as much blood on Jack's leg as he expected.

Jack eased himself into the driver's seat. His leg hurt; not excessive pain, just as if he had three inches of kitchen knife sticking out. He had to move as far as he could to the left to avoid pushing the knife in further when he shut the door. At least he was still *compos mentis*; one concern he had, especially if he was driving, was if he fainted. Best keep the speed down.

He started the engine, set up the satnav for the quickest way to the hospital and slowly pulled away. These roads here were quiet, and would give him a chance to get used to this before he reached the main road.

He was taken along a couple of quiet residential streets to the main road, which he crossed over to enter another quiet residential street, which took him as far as Dalston Lane. He had a rough idea of where he was now: he was sure Hackney Downs station was along to the right.

He was correct. The satnav took him on a right turn, and past Hackney Downs station, third exit on the roundabout into Dalston Lane. He knew where he was headed: along Dalston Lane, Lower

Clapton Road and into Homerton High Street. The hospital was just off the High Street.

He was correct in his anticipation, except that the satnav took him along a couple of little side streets to Homerton Row, which runs parallel to the High Street. This is where the hospital is situated. 'Thank God for that,' he said aloud as he slowly turned into the car park. His leg was starting to throb, and was beginning to feel slightly numb around his foot. Whether that was because of the knife or his *Bag for Life* tourniquet, he couldn't tell. He was sure having to continually move his right leg to press on the brake and gas couldn't have helped.

He parked, and found himself limping across to the Accident & Emergency entrance. He tried not to look too conspicuous, his coat partially covering the knife. He walked in and looked around. It was busy. There were at least a couple of dozen people sitting waiting to be seen, and a queue of four waiting to see a nurse who was sitting on a stool at a raised desk. Jack assumed that was some kind of triage, so he joined the queue. He was surprised he was still able to stand up. It was then that the triage nurse seemed to notice the knife sticking out of Jack's leg. She picked up the phone on her little desk and made a call. Within a minute, a male nurse appeared and walked over to Jack.

'Hey there,' the nurse said, taking Jack's elbow and putting an arm around his waist. 'I think you'd better come through here with me.' Jack made no objection and let the nurse lead him through a set of double doors, along a short corridor and into a side room. 'Here,' the nurse said, taking Jack over to the bed. 'I'll just get you on -'

It was then that Jack fainted.

CHAPTER NINETEEN

AS IT TURNED out, he had only been out for a few seconds.

When Jack came to, he was lying on the examination bed. The male nurse who had brought him into the room was raising his right leg, and a female nurse was putting a blanket over him.

'This will keep you warm,' the nurse said. 'In case you go into shock.'

'And I've raised your leg,' her colleague said, 'just to control the blood flow.' He looked down at Jack's home-made tourniquet. 'We'll leave that on until Doctor gets here.'

'Did I faint?' Jack asked.

'You did for a few seconds, yes.'

'Jesus Christ, what a wuss,' Jack exclaimed, then looked at the female nurse. 'Sorry.'

She smiled. 'Nothing to be sorry for. Now you just lie here and wait for the doctor.'

'Would you like a drink?' the male nurse asked. 'Tea? Hot and sweet.'

'I'd prefer a coffee,' Jack said.

The two nurses glanced at each other.

'Tea's better,' the nurse said as she adjusted the blanket. Alex will get it for you.'

'Back in a jiff,' Alex said, and left the room.

Just as Alex left, a young woman walked in. Jack guessed she was the doctor as she was wearing dark blue scrubs, as opposed to the light blue Alex and his colleague were wearing. She was short, and her jet black hair was tied in a tight and neat bun.

'I'm Dr Bakshi,' she said by way of introduction. 'And you are?' She looked over at the nurse as she asked.

'The patient fainted,' the nurse explained, 'so we've not had time to -'

'The patient's name is Jack,' said Jack. 'Jack Richardson.'

Dr Bakshi nodded. 'Okay. I think the priority is to get this out, deal with the wound, and get Mr Richardson's details then. Is that okay with you,

Mr Richardson?'

'Just call me Jack. Mr Richardson's a bit of a mouthful.' Jack found the doctor very attractive and he wished he had phrased his last sentence better.

The doctor leaned over and looked at the knife. 'Do you know if the edges are serrated?'

'They're not. What you see there is what's inside my leg.'

'Can you feel your leg?'

'Yes, perfectly. A little too perfectly, actually,' he winced.

'Can you walk? How did you get here?'

'Yes, I can walk. And drive.'

'You drove here? How far?'

'Only London Fields.'

'You drove with that knife sticking out of your leg?'

'I did. I recall reading somewhere that I shouldn't take it out.'

In the meantime, Alex returned with a mug of steaming tea. 'Here you are, love. I'll leave it on here.' He put the mug on a side table.

'No, you shouldn't,' said Dr Bakshi. 'You shouldn't drive either. We're going to have to cut your trousers to get to the wound. Is there someone who could bring another pair in?'

'Not in this part of London. Couldn't you just cut a little kind of flap around the knife?'

The doctor checked the area again. 'Yes, I suppose we could do that. Probably need about ten by ten centimetres. Would that be all right?'

Jack grimaced. He was thinking how much the trousers cost. 'Yeah, all right. Go on then.'

'I'm going to cut that flap, then give you a local anaesthetic before we pull the knife out. How much of the blade is in your leg? Not much, I would guess.'

'I saw it before it went in, so two, three inches tops.'

'Was it an accident?'

'Er… kind of.'

'Kind of? Are you going to report it to the police?'

'I hadn't thought.' He paused. 'You should have seen the other fella,' he laughed.

She nodded. 'That's up to you, then. The hospital isn't under any obligation to report stab wounds. Ones such as this, at any rate.'

'I was surprised how little blood there is. I suppose it'll bleed more when you pull the knife out.'

'I suspect it hasn't hit any major blood vessels. Just body fat.'

'Muscle, you mean?'

She laughed. 'Maybe some muscle. Are you limping much?'

'A little.'

'If it's a little, then I suspect there's not much muscle damage either. Just a flesh wound, you might say.'

'That sounds better than body fat,' Jack laughed, staring the doctor on the face. He realised at that point he was trying to flirt with her.

'Indeed,' she replied. 'So, we'll give you the anaesthetic, take the knife, stem any bleeding, and sterilise the wound, and seal it. Then we'll take you down to x-ray just to check there isn't any internal damage. Is that okay with you? There's also some paperwork to do, and some you'll need to sign before we start.'

Dr Bakshi left the room; almost immediately the other nurse returned with a clipboard. 'I just need to take some details,' she said. 'Oh, you've not touched your tea,' she added, passing the now lukewarm cup to Jack. She helped him to sit up so he could drink the tea without spilling it.

'Thanks,' Jack said. 'I didn't get your name, by the way.'

'Lucy.'

'Thanks, Lucy.'

'You're welcome. Now...'

For the next five minutes, Lucy asked a number of questions: name, address, date of birth, blood group, allergies, in particular to anaesthetic; even next of kin, which made Jack feel a little less blasé.

'Doctor says you're not going to the police about this,' she said. 'Is that right?'

'Yes, that's right. It was an accident. My stupid fault.'

'O-kay,' she said slowly. Jack could see she was scoring through a whole section on her proforma. 'I'll just need you to sign here,' she said, passing the clipboard to him, 'to give your consent to the procedure.'

Jack signed and lay back on the bed. Lucy smiled, looked over the document and said, 'Doctor will be back soon.'

Jack lay there, waiting, with his knees raised. He thought it a rather strange sight, a kitchen knife sticking out of his upper leg. He recalled the doctor had ignored his homemade tourniquet.

After a few more minutes, Dr Bakshi returned, this time with a pair of scissors and a needle. 'Tell me if this hurts,' she said, as she slowly cut a hole in his trouser leg. She cut three sides, allowing the cut material to hang down. Then she pressed the plunger to expel any air bubbles and, gave Jack the injection. 'It will take about ten minutes to become fully effective. Alex will stay with you. Don't forget your tea.'

'Does it hurt?' Alex paused and looked at Jack.

'My leg doesn't, but my wallet does. I just

remembered how much I paid for these.'

'You could ask your wife to sew the patch back,' Alex joked. 'Or are you single?'

'Divorced. No, it's all right; I'll cope.'

'Your tea,' Alex said. 'Don't forget it.'

'I won't.' Jack took a sip, realised the tea was lukewarm, so finished the whole cup. 'Apparently it's a flesh wound,' he said to Alex, pointing down at the knife.

Alex nodded. 'That's why there's not much blood. But when she pulls the knife out, I'll have a cloth at the ready in case it bleeds more. The knife might have been plugging a hole. An accident, was it?' he asked, giving Jack the look a parent would give a child when they disbelieved something they were told.

Jack nodded. He had the feeling Alex knew it was no accident. 'You should have seen the other guy,' he repeated.

Alex grinned and rested a hand on Jack's shoulder. 'Say no more,' he mouthed.

'I still can't believe I fainted,' Jack said, closing his eyes.

'Don't worry.' Alex put his hand on Jack's shoulder again. 'It happens to everyone.'

Dr Bakshi returned, this time with Lucy, who was pushing a small aluminium trolley, on which were three rolls of bandage. Both were wearing blue latex gloves. The doctor put two fingers on

Jack's leg, either side of the knife, and pressed. 'Can you feel that?' she asked.

Jack shook his head.

Dr Bakshi nodded. 'Right' she said to Lucy.

Lucy then took one of the rolls of bandage, unwrapped around two feet, and put it on Jack's leg, around the knife. 'This is to soak up any blood,' she explained.

'Here goes,' Dr Bakshi said. She put two fingers of her left hand on the bandages, and used the other hand to slowly ease the knife out of Jack's leg. He could feel something, movement, but no pain.

It took two seconds to fully extract the knife. Jack had been correct in his assumption: there had been three inches of knife in his leg, but there was very little blood on the blade.

'Much blood?' he asked Lucy, who was attending to the wound.

She shook her head.

'Now, we're going to clean the wound, then seal it up,' the doctor said. Once Lucy had cleaned it, Dr Bakshi sealed it. The blade, and therefore the wound, were less than an inch in width, and the doctor needed only one sterile strip to do the job. She stuck one end of the strip one side of the wound, pushed both sides of the gash together, then stuck the strip down the other side. 'There may be some swelling,' she said, 'but that's normal. The steri-strip is elastic, so will stretch. But if you get worried about it, come back and see us. Or your local hospital. Before you leave, we'll make an out-patient appointment for you, just to check over how you're doing. The strip itself will fall off on its own in seven to ten days. Don't pick at it or rub it, and try and keep it dry. Don't go swimming or have a bath, and if you take a shower, cover it with -' She tugged at his *Bag for Life* tourniquet. 'Something like that. And don't shower for too long.'

'My tourniquet?' Jack asked.

The doctor smiled. 'I guessed it was something like that.'

'Did it do any good?' he asked.

'Maybe,' she laughed. 'It's not very tight, though. I'll take it off.' She picked up the scissors they had used to cut Jack's trouser leg, and snipped through the plastic bag, which they discarded with the used bandages. 'Now, we just need to get you down to x-ray. I'm pretty confident you're fixed now, but we'll need to make sure there was no internal damage.'

'Okay,' Jack said, and started to get off the bed.

'No, no, no,' Lucy said. 'Wheelchair.'

'You're kidding,' Jack said. 'I drove here.'

Alex had reappeared and brought the wheelchair over and helped Jack into it.

'Are you planning on driving home?' Dr Bakshi asked.

'I was planning on that.'

'There's nobody who could take you home?'

'Not in this part of town. In any case, my car's in your car park, being charged hundreds of pounds an hour.'

Dr Bakshi sighed. 'Let's get the x-ray done, and we'll see how you are then. It does appear to have been only a flesh wound.'

Jack looked up at Alex, who had begun to push the wheelchair. 'She means muscle.'

'I'm sure of that, love,' Alex said, pushing Jack into the corridor. Jack folded over the flap in his trousers, and got wheeled down to x-ray, hoping that he would not bump into anybody who knew him.

CHAPTER TWENTY

THE X-RAY WAS fine. It was, as Dr Bakshi had said, a flesh wound. Fifty-four millimetres of the blade, seventeen millimetres at its widest, reducing to a point. It had missed all major blood vessels. A little bit of muscle had been damaged, but nothing that would not heal given time and rest.

Alex had parked Jack's wheelchair in the waiting room of the x-ray department. While he was waiting for one of the x-ray staff to wheel him in, he tried walking. He got up out of the wheelchair without any difficulty, and was able to walk three or four times up and down the waiting room.

'Mr Richardson?' a nurse called out. Jack returned to the wheelchair for her to take him into the other room. 'How does the leg feel? she asked.

'It's starting to get a bit sore, to be honest. Beginning to throb. Maybe I shouldn't have tried walking.'

'It's probably the anaesthetic wearing off. That's normal. We'll give you some painkillers before you go, assuming there's nothing untoward on the x-ray.'

Which there wasn't. They gave him the results of the x-ray, repeated the instruction not to fiddle with the strips, or get them wet, and they would fall off of their own accord after about a week. He had a week's supply of painkillers, one four times a day, and to call if they needed replenishing. Avoid alcohol with them, as it causes drowsiness. He would be contacted by text about a follow-up appointment, which would be at his local hospital. The doctor asked how he was getting home, and grimaced slightly when Jack said he was driving.

It was four fifteen now, and the rush hour was about to begin. Jack did consider going to the hospital café to get a coffee and maybe something to eat just to pass the time until the rush hour was over, but that would mean waiting here till around seven, and not getting home till half eight.

He walked up and down the hospital corridor a few times: his leg seemed fine. It ached a little; maybe it was time for another painkiller. He bought himself a double expresso and took another tramadol, then walked, slightly slower than normal, to the hospital car park. He could see the traffic on the main road as he waited in line to pay for his parking. It was busy, and would get more so. That might be to his advantage: there would be more traffic, but it would be moving more slowly.

He was right: the traffic was slow, not much over twenty. This suited Jack, and he kept to that speed, making sure there was extra distance between him and the car in front. If the vehicle behind got too close, he would lightly touch the brake pedal, just so they kept their distance.

He got indoors, unscathed, at just after six. His leg was aching a bit more now, probably down to the physical effort of pressing on the car pedals. Too early for another painkiller; no more than one every four hours they told him. And no alcohol!

He made himself another coffee, then crashed down onto his sofa. He was tired, much more than he normally would be this time of day. Maybe it was delayed shock; maybe it was the effects of the painkillers. He leaned his head back and closed his eyes, then took three mouthfuls of the black coffee.

Now, of course, he would have to tell people: Cathy, and by extension, Mel; Susan, and work. He would call Mike Smith first.

Jack reached over to his phone and speed-dialled Mike.

'Jack. I was just thinking about you.'

'Oh yes? In what context?'

'That assignment you're on and how you were getting on. Remember you've got till tomorrow evening.'

'Yeah, well; that's why I'm calling.'

'Developments?'

'You could say that. I went back down to London Fields first thing. I wanted to speak with some of the neighbours, people who lived in the block, to try to get some background on the victim.'

'How did you get on?'

'Well, firstly I was able to speak to two or three people who lived in the block. They knew the family, and all of them said that the boy wasn't the poor innocent victim I'd assumed he was.'

'Oh? In what way?'

'They all spoke of him, and other youths continually hanging around the block or the Green outside. One of the women said she and her granddaughter felt threatened. And they were smoking something that wasn't a cigarette.'

'So you're saying that he wasn't the innocent victim, being in the wrong place at the wrong time?'

'Quite possibly not. But that's not all. After I'd done, I was walking back to the car and was approached by two guys I had spoken to the last time I went down there. That time I spoke to them, they were sitting on one of the benches on the Green, smoking something, that also wasn't a cigarette.'

'They approached you?'

'Yes. They told me basically to stay the fuck away, then one of them stabbed me.'

'What? You've been stabbed? Where are you now? What…?'

'It's okay. I'm back home now.'

'You've been to hospital? Where?'

'The local one. Homerton, I think. It was only five minutes' drive from where it happened.'

'You drove? Jesus. After you'd been stabbed? Where'd he stab you?'

'It was in the leg. Upper leg. A flesh wound, the doctor said. Not much blood.'

'They fixed it?'

'They pulled out the knife – it was a six inch kitchen knife – cleaned up the wound and sewed it up.'

'Six inches?'

'Yeah, but only half the blade went in.'

'Ouch, anyway.'

'Yeah, so they sewed it up, rather put those sticky strips on, gave me an x-ray to check there was no internal damage, which there wasn't, and sent me home.'

'And you drove home? Jesus. How are you feeling now?'

'Very tired. My leg ached like hell after the drive; you know, brake pedal, gas pedal, up and down. And I've had I think it's three doses of painkillers.'

'Are you planning on calling in sick?'

'I wasn't planning on that. But it's up to you, Mike. You gave me until tomorrow evening to make progress on this story. I think I've made some, but there again I could go off sick and carry on, on my own time.'

'How are you going to get around? Surely you're not planning on driving.'

'I'll just have to use the tube. Probably easier to get around that way, anyway. The thing is, Mike, I've obviously hit a raw nerve somewhere. All I did was ask around for a back story on some supposedly innocent kid. Why would I need to get warned off, with a kitchen knife at that?'

There was silence on the other end of the line, which meant that Mike was ruminating.

'All right; keep at it. We'll talk at the end of the week; agree next steps then.'

'Two more days.'

'Yes, two more days, but the end of the week seems a logical time to review progress. Are you going to the police about this? You should do; it could have been a lot worse.'

'That's what the doctors asked. I said no, but I'll think about it. What I'm thinking is this: these guys have to be part of what I'm looking for. If I do go to the police, they're either going to get arrested, or they'll disappear, and that's the end of the lead. I'll keep that as an option for now. By the way, I think one of them's got a broken nose.'

'Why do you say that?'

'I broke it.'

'What with?'

'My head.'

Mike laughed. 'Of course, you could always get a couple of your mates to kick the shit out of them.'

'That thought did occur to me.'

'Jack, it was a joke. If you want retribution, go to the police.'

'I will, yes.'

'Do your family know?'

'I'm about to ring them.'

'I'll let you get on then. I'd better call Martin, let him know. He might call you himself; he might not.'

'I'm trembling with anticipation.'

'Speak Friday, Jack. And take it easy, for Christ's sake.'

'I will.'

Jack ended the call and prepared for the next. He had to call Susan, and Cathy, who he knew would pass the phone over to her mother, and that meant Jack having to explain three times what happened. He also knew they would all express shock and want to fuss; to reprimand him for not calling them for help (what could they have done, anyway?) and for driving himself home. Then the exhortations to be careful, to take some time off to recover. That he should go to the police. And so on and so on. Then offers to come over to see him, God forbid in Mel's case, not so much in the others' – but he was fine on his own here. He was, however, more than aware that it could have been a lot worse. His joke to the doctor about you should have seen the other fella was true, but it could easily have gone the other way. This was the first time in his career that he had been assaulted, and he had to admit, it had shaken him up. Not that he would admit that to anyone. He would just chill out, take it easy, and continue with the story as best he could. At least the deadline had been extended.

He called his daughter first. Then Susan.

Both calls went exactly as he had expected, including Cathy passing the phone over to her mother. He was fine. It was only a flesh wound. Yes, he knew it could have been worse. You should have seen the other guy. Yes, I am taking it seriously. No, I'm not taking any unnecessary risks. You don't need to come over. You really don't. Please don't. I'll be fine to have Cathy at the weekend. Then: I'm fine, it was only a flesh wound. Yes, it could have been worse. No, I'm not driving for a couple of days; going to rest the leg. It would be great if you came over tomorrow, if your mother can babysit. I understand you can't spend the night. No, it won't affect that, although you might have to be on top.

After the calls, it took ten minutes and some pain to pull off the cut trousers, which went into the bin. He fixed himself some scrambled eggs, changed into a tee-shirt and shorts, then lay down on the bed. He didn't feel he needed any more painkillers right now. What he and his leg needed was rest.

Vowing to get back to the story the next morning, Jack quickly drifted off to sleep.

CHAPTER TWENTY-ONE

JACK WOKE AT just after four. His leg ached slightly. Not hurting, just an ache.

He decided against taking another painkiller for now, and to wait until around seven or eight.

He noticed as he checked the time on his phone that a text message had come through while he was asleep. At 22:56, to be precise. He thought he recognised the number.

Hi, i heard wot happened ru ok?

It had to be the boy Levi, to whom he spoke the other day. He was about to reply, then dropped the phone on the bedside table. He would reply when he got up, not at four in the morning. If he started chatting on there now, he would never get to sleep, and would feel like crap all day.

He was soon back to sleep.

He reflected how tired he had been, or how strong the tramadol was, when he woke at eight forty-five, feeling much refreshed. He was a bit twitchy about taking a shower in view of what the doctor had said, so just washed his face, postponing having a shower until later, for when Susan arrived.

He dressed and looked at his phone. Talk of the devil: he had had a message from Susan.

Morning, just checking you're okay. Be round at 6 tonight, straight from work. Will bring in dinner x

He replied, **Perfect. See you at 6 x.**

He made himself a coffee, and looked once more at the message from Levi. Interesting, he mused, before replying.

Am good, tx. Would like to talk some more – are you free today?

He was waiting for the toaster to finish when his phone pinged. He quickly stepped over, then groaned when he saw who it was from. It was from Martin Fineman, who was the paper's

Editor, and Mike Smith's boss. Mike had obviously just told him, and did tell Jack when they spoke, to expect a call. This was about as personal as you could get from Fineman, which suited Jack anyway. The message was on the lines of how sorry he was to hear of what had happened, how he hoped Jack was all right, and that he would recover quickly.

'"Recover quickly". Fucking idiot,' Jack muttered, putting the phone back on the table, but as he turned, it pinged again. This was what Jack was wanting to see: a reply from Levi.

Can talk but not on here, meet somewhere away from e8

Jack replied, **Absolutely. Where and when?**

Could you meet me Paddington station at 11?

'Paddington?' Jack said aloud. **Where in Paddington?** he asked.

Outside the Smiths bookstore?

Good for me. See you there 11am.

Jack tapped his chin with his phone, as he did when thinking. Why did Levi want to get so far away from home to talk? And why face to face, and not on the phone? Strange; but he'd soon find out. Getting down to Paddington would not be that onerous: he would not need to drive – it would just be a matter of limping down to the Tube station, then one change at Kings Cross. It was not nine thirty, so it would be time to leave soon. He needed to get there before eleven.

It was actually ten thirty-five when he was slowly walking down the steps from the bridge which leads from the Hammersmith & City part of the station down to between Platforms 8 and 9 of the main part. He slowly made his way past the cycle parking and the main station concourse. The WHSmith bookshop was across the concourse. No sign of Levi, but there were still twenty minutes to go. He bought himself a cappuccino and stood by the ticket machines, watching the store entrance. His leg was not too bad; he had taken a painkiller before he left home, and it was not so bad, provided he didn't walk too fast.

At ten fifty-four Levi appeared. He stopped outside the bookstore, looking around: Jack assumed that was for him. He seemed ill at ease, and this did not change when Jack walked up to him.

'Hey,' Jack said.

Still shifting from foot to foot, Levi muttered, 'Hey.'

'You want a coffee or something?' Jack asked, holding up his paper cup.

'Nah, I'm good,' Levi replied, then adding, 'No, I'll have a coke.'

'One coke,' Jack said. He looked into the store

and saw there was a chiller cabinet containing bottled drinks, sweets, snacks and sandwiches. 'One coke,' he repeated as they stepped over to the cabinet. 'Regular or diet?'

'Regular's good,' replied Levi, both hands in his pockets.

Jack extracted the bottle and took it over to the self-service point. As he scanned the bottle, he casually looked back to make sure Levi was still there. Handing him the bottle, Jack asked, 'Where do you want to go?'

Levi looked around. 'Somewhere quiet.'

'There's plenty of seats upstairs,' Jack said, using his paper cup to point up to the mezzanine level, where there were a couple of food stands, plus plenty of empty seats.

Levi nodded. 'That's cool.' They took one of the escalators up to the mezzanine and easily found two seats away from everybody else.

'This is an odd place to meet, yes?' Jack said. 'Why here? Not an easy journey.'

Levi shook his head. 'I just go to Liverpool Street, then the Elizabeth Line here.'

'Ah, right. Easier for you than me.'

'How is your leg?'

'It hurts a bit. They gave me painkillers. I'm not driving for a few days. The hospital says it was just a flesh wound, so I suppose I was lucky. You seen the guys who did it?'

'One of them. He's got a huge plaster across here.' Levi ran a finger across his face. 'His nose looks an odd shape. Did you break it?'

'Looks like it,' Jack said. 'Did he go to a hospital?'

'Don't know. It's probably an improvement: he was an ugly cunt, anyway.' Levi grinned.

'I haven't decided whether to go to the police yet. I'm still thinking about it.'

Levi said nothing: just used the arm of the seat to remove the bottle top and took a mouthful of coke.

'So,' Jack said, 'you wanted to talk to me.'

'No, that's what you said,' said Levi.

'Yes,' Jack conceded. 'I went down to London Fields yesterday.'

'I know that,' Levi said, pointing to Jack's legs. 'Which leg was it?'

'This one,' Jack said, tapping where the knife went in. 'Ouch. That was dumb.'

'Yeah, it was,' Levi grinned, sipping more coke.

'Anyway,' Jack continued, 'when I went down there I spoke to a few of the neighbours, people who live in the same block as Navindra.' He paused a second. 'Do you live in that block? Are you one of the neighbours?'

Levi shook his head. 'Nah. My place is Haggerston way. Near Cambridge Heath.'

'With your family?'

'No. I share a house with three others.'

'So why did I first see you hanging around London Fields?'

'It's hardly the other side of the world. There's a little park there, but not much going on.'

'The guys you were with: how'd you come to know them?'

Levi shrugged. 'Just by hanging around.'

Jack took the last mouthful of cappuccino and wiped his mouth with his hand. 'The neighbours I spoke to,' he said, 'all said that he was always hanging about the Green with other guys. A couple of the neighbours said they found him intimidating; or rather, the group. One said she was in that little swing park – you know where I mean?'

'Yeah, I know it.'

'She said she was sitting there watching her grandkid on the swing or slide or whatever, and Navindra and some others were standing right behind her. Behind some railings, but directly behind her. Just watching. She felt so intimidated she took her grandkid back home.'

Levi drank some more coke. He looked from side to side. 'You want to know about him?' he asked. 'I can tell you about him.'

CHAPTER TWENTY-TWO

LEVI HELD OUT his hand. 'How much?' he asked.

'How much what?'

'How much you going to give me for the lowdown on Nav?'

'Depend how much you have to tell me.'

Levi said nothing.

'Okay,' said Jack. 'We'll start at fifty; if what you have to tell me is really useful, I'll make it seventy-five.'

'Deal.' Levi looked Jack in the eye and kept his hand out. Jack felt into his back pocket, took out his wallet and gave Levi two twenties and a ten. Leroy hurriedly pocketed the cash. Jack's eyes darted around to check they were not being watched. He could imagine what an observer might have inferred from a middle-aged man giving a twenty-something a wad of cash in the middle of Paddington station.

'Now,' Jack said. 'Tell me about Navindra Dhabi.'

Levi finished his coke, suppressed a belch, and took a deep breath. 'You must have heard of the E8s?'

'The E8 gang? Yes, I've heard of them. Are you a member?'

'Yeah,' Levi replied, slightly shiftily. 'Me and some others.'

'Was he?'

'He was.' He looked around before continuing. 'Do you know what gangs like the E8 do?'

'Fight other gangs?'

'Well, that happens. But we just hang out. There's nothing else to do, man. We just hang out together.'

'I see. So where does the E8 gang *hang out*?'

'Just around the E8 area. Our turf, our territory. We stick to that. That's when the fighting happens; when gangs have their territory invaded.'

'Is that what happened that night? The Kings invaded your territory?'

'Yeah, that's what happened. They arrived,

and started to swan down the High Street, like they owned the place. So we had to defend our borders, didn't we? It's our manor.'

'Which is why they got chased down the High Street and over to the Green?'

'How'd you know that? Was you there?'

'I've also spoken to a couple of guys from the Kings. Anyway, I wasn't asking about what happened then; I was asking you about Navindra. Tell me about him. By the way, they hadn't come over just to invade your manor, as you put it: apparently one of them had some business to do with one of your gang.'

'Oh,' said Levi. He seemed surprised. 'That might be true.'

'You're being very opaque.'

'What does that mean?'

'You're not being very clear. Come on, I've given you fifty quid, maybe there's more coming your way. But you need to tell me stuff.'

Levi nodded. 'Okay. This is how it is. Gangs hang out, like I said, because there's nothing to do. Most of us don't have a job, so we have to get hold of money somewhere. So we work for people. We move money and shit around for them.'

'You're into money laundering?'

'Sometimes. Other times… You know what biscuits are?'

'Fuck,' said Jack. 'You people are distributing ecstasy?'

'Not just that. Snow too.'

'What's that?'

'Cocaine.'

'How do you do that?'

'You seen those guys outside shops? In a sleeping bag? Plastic cup or something for cash?'

'I have, yes.'

'The cash that goes in there is the payment. Then somewhere else, it's the snow or the biscuits that go in there.'

Jack leaned back and nodded. 'I get it. They're everywhere; so much so they're almost invisible.'

'Yeah, 'cause most people don't wanna know. They just want to walk past.'

'So that's how you do it. But what's that got to do with the Kings?'

'Sometimes a gang has cash to pass on. So that gets passed to another gang to pass to another gang, maybe another, and so on. The more times it's passed on, the harder it is for the cops to follow it.'

'So the cash you pass on, is that all from drugs? Or other stuff?'

'Not all. If a store gets done over, or someone gets shaken down.'

'Who would you get shaken down?'

Levi sniggered. 'Guys like you, mostly. You

married?'

'Divorced. What's that got to do with it?'

'But you was married, right? Guys like you, married, want a bit on the side, you know what I mean?'

'They get that from you, is that what you're saying? You're the bit on the side?'

'Me and some others.'

'Including Nav?'

'He did sometimes, yeah.'

'How did you…?'

'How did we meet the punters, you mean? You heard of Grindr?'

'Heard of, never actually…'

Levi laughed. 'Of course not, pal. It's on there. Grindr, BoyZone, Hornet. I mainly use BoyZone. Under a different name, of course. Levi's my real name. Anyway, we arrange to meet someone, they have to be married or with someone. Also over thirty; twenty-somethings don't have the money. I meet them somewhere; not my place, or his, or even a hotel. Some of them want to go to a hotel. In a car, bit of wasteland, round the back of somewhere, and let them fuck me. A hundred quid is the normal price for a fuck, fifty for a blow. But what they don't know is that someone else is videoing it. Then the guy gets sent a few seconds of the video, and…'

'And you tell him you'll send the video to his

wife unless they pay up.'

'Pretty much, yes. I can earn a grand a week, at least.'

'And it all goes to you?'

'No, I have to give some to the gang leader.'

'And what's his name?'

'Sorry, pal. No can do.'

Jack shrugged. 'So that's what Navindra did? Ran drug money and blackmailed married men?' He squinted at Levi. 'And you actually enjoy doing that?'

'I'll admit, some of the creeps are disgusting. Old, fat, dirty; but for a hundred a time, it's all right. If they're really ugly or fat, then I'll charge more. They never last for long, anyway. Anything else you want to know? I need to go in a minute.'

'No; I think I've got the picture.'

Levi stood up. 'I'll be off then. Thanks for the fifty.'

'An easier way to earn than usual, I expect?' said Jack, looking up at him.

'Probably. Maybe I'll see you around? But then, you'll know you're on camera, won't you?'

Jack nodded. 'I will, yes.'

'Hope your leg gets better.'

With that, Levi turned, and left. Jack watched him as he went down the escalator and across the concourse to his train back.

Interesting, he thought. Again, so Navindra wasn't the innocent bystander; that was becoming obvious. Or was it? The fact that when he wasn't loitering around London Fields, he was doing tricks for married men didn't mean that he wasn't an innocent bystander that night.

Then again, if he, like Levi, was blackmailing the men he met, that could be a whole different scenario.

But where did that leave Jaylon? He was still found next to Navindra's body, covered in his blood.

Jack pushed himself off the seat. His leg was beginning to ache a little. It was probably time to get off home, before the tube got busy, and getting a seat would be difficult. He took the escalator down to the platform, the same as Levi had done a few moments earlier, then began the slow walk along the platform and up the steps to the Hammersmith & City platforms.

A not entirely unsuccessful conversation, he felt. He had got some answers, after all.

But those answers now raised another set of questions.

CHAPTER TWENTY-THREE

JACK HAD JUST taken some more painkillers when Susan knocked on his door. He swallowed the water with a gulp, then half walked, half limped down the hallway. Maybe two-thirds walk, one third limp was more accurate; either his leg was getting better, or the painkillers were fast acting. He did think about how easier it would have been if she had a key, but had never even considered giving her one. He did not have a key to her place, either; they had not even discussed that. That would indicate the relationship moving to the next level: going for a drink, sex, unprotected sex, exchanging of door keys. Where did meeting the family and friends come into the equation? They had done neither, and Jack was happy with that. She seemed to be as well, so he figured there was no reason to rock the boat.

'Hey, hey,' he said, as he held the door open for her.

'How you doing?' she asked, brushing past, pausing to kiss him and holding up a large white plastic bag. 'I brought dinner.'

'Takeaway?' he asked as he followed her into the kitchen.

'Not exactly. Ready meal. I didn't feel like cooking properly, and I suspect you won't have much in the way of fresh stuff here. No, you don't,' she added, quickly checking his fridge.

'What have we got?' Jack asked, as Susan unpacked her white bag.

She read out the labels from each packet. 'Beef Bourguignon, with vegetables, and Dauphinoise Potatoes, followed by chocolate pudding.'

'Nice.'

'I thought you'd appreciate the chocolate pudding. Oh, and a bottle of this.' She held up a bottle of Californian Merlot.

'Ah,' said Jack. 'I hope you like that. I'm on painkillers; I can't drink.'

'Oh, shit. I hadn't thought of that.'

'And you drove here?'

'No, I got a cab, so I could enjoy this. You

being on painkillers never entered my head.'

'Sorry; what you don't drink we can keep for another night. Are you…?'

'Am I staying over? Not tonight. I'd love to, and my mother's taking Kyle to school in the morning; but I've got an early start. I'd need to get a cab home, then get ready for work, then drive to the office. It'd just be too rushed and complicated, and would probably mean setting the alarm for five AM. In any case, don't you need to rest?'

'Only my leg. The rest of me doesn't.' As he spoke, he pulled her up against him; she put her arms around his neck, and they enjoyed a long, passionate kiss. She could feel him through their clothes.

'So I see,' she laughed, pulling away. 'Let me get this food started, then you can tell me what happened.'

The food needed thirty-five minutes. She insisted on waiting until Jack's oven had warmed up, and once the beef was inside, they sat on his sofa. He poured her a large glass of Merlot, and took a coke for himself.

'So,' she said. 'Your leg. Somebody stabbed you. How did that happen?'

'It was a kitchen knife, around this long.' He held up his hands, his index fingers demonstrating. 'The blade was six inches I suppose, and only half went in.'

'Not serrated, I hope?'

'No, fortunately. I took myself to the local hospital, they took the knife out, cleaned up the wound, sealed it, gave me painkillers. They also gave me an x-ray to check there had been no internal damage.'

'And had there?'

'No, just a flesh wound, the doctor said. There wasn't much blood either; well, not from me.'

'What do you mean?'

'One of the other guys – I think I broke his nose. Plenty of blood there.'

'How did you do that?'

Jack put a finger on his forehead. 'With this.'

'I see.' She paused as she took a sip of wine. 'Hold on: you said you took yourself to hospital. Which hospital?'

'I think it's called Homerton General. Only five minutes away.'

'How did you get there?'

'In the car, how else?'

'With a knife sticking out of your leg?'

'It was okay. Only five minutes away.'

'And how did you get back here yesterday?'

'In the car.'

'You drove all that way - in the rush hour, yes? - just after having a knife taken out of your leg. And dopey with painkillers, I suppose?'

'It was okay. I didn't rush. And I got back in one piece.'

'Why didn't you call me? I could have met you there and driven you back here.'

'I did think of calling someone - you, or one of the guys at work - but it would have been difficult logistically, and you have Kyle to think about.'

She shook her head. 'Even so, I could have worked something out.'

'Okay, okay; I will next time.'

'It could have been worse, Jack.'

'I know that.'

'Tell me how it happened.'

Jack took a deep breath, drained his glass of coke, and talked about his visit to London Fields the day before. She sat quietly listening, taking the occasional sip of wine. She occasionally shook her head slightly.

'Jesus, Jack, you need to be more careful. You're putting yourself at risk.'

'I can look after myself; didn't I show that yesterday?'

'Yes, but what if there had been three of them? Or a different type of knife? Or if one of them had a gun?'

Jack said nothing; just nodded. She was right.

The food was ready now, so Jack laid the table while Susan dished up. Another glass of Merlot for Susan; another coke for Jack.

'So have you been here all day?' she asked as they ate.

'No, I've been across to Paddington. I didn't drive before you ask.' He then related to her his conversation with Levi.

'He's a rent boy, then?' she asked.

'I hadn't thought about it in those terms, but yes; I suppose he is. He says he's on a couple of websites; no, apps.' He took a mouthful of coke. 'I'm going to change this for water,' he said, trying to stand up.

'I'll get it, Susan said. 'I'll be quicker.'

'Thanks,' Jack said as she returned to the table with a glass of tap water. 'Does the name John Porter mean anything to you?'

'John Porter? No, the name doesn't ring any bells? Why? Should I know him?'

'Not necessarily. He was an MP - just an MP, I think; I don't think he was a Minister or anything – and had to resign his seat after he had been caught up in sleaze.'

She shook her head. 'Still doesn't mean anything.'

'He was exposed meeting up with rent boys, male prostitutes and the like.'

'Exposed? In the papers, you mean?'

'Initially.'

'Your paper?'

'Yup.'

'By you?'

'Yes, by me. And a couple of my colleagues. We were doing a feature about corruption and sleaze in Parliament, and he was definitely on our radar. He liked fresh meat, shall we say.'

'How old was he?'

'Fifties, I think.'

Susan pulled a face. 'Horrible. Dirty old men.'

'Well, that's the type of clientele Levi has. People who are vulnerable to blackmail. He says another guy videos it, unbeknown to the punter, who then gets blackmailed.'

'Who videos it?'

'Another member of the E8s.'

'Obviously very lucrative.'

'Yes, he said he only sees men over thirty.'

'Who are most likely to be in a long term relationship, with children, a home, a mortgage, all that.'

'And who have the most to lose.'

'It was interesting about how they passed the proceeds on.'

'Using homeless people, you mean? Or rather, people pretending to be homeless.'

'That's right. You see them everywhere in London, don't you? But nobody notices them.'

'People try not to; that's the point. Hiding in plain sight.'

'What you were saying about those men being videoed having sex…'

'Yes, from a distance and in secret.'

'That's not what I meant.' As she spoke, she laid her hand on Jack's. 'Is that something you have ever done?'

He squeezed her hand as he replied. 'My ex and I did it once, years ago. When we were first together.' He omitted to say that he had done it several times since, with several other women, but decided that was too much information to share.

'I see,' she said, finishing her glass of wine. 'Maybe when your leg is better.'

'Yes. Maybe. Cheers.' He raised his glass of tap water.

After they had finished their meal, Jack said he wanted to take a shower before they did anything else. Although she hadn't said as much, he was sure Susan had not come over straight from work; she had to go home first to drop her car off, and smelt like she had taken a shower before coming over. He was conscious of the fact that he had not showered since the previous morning; only a brief face wash today.

'You go ahead,' she said. 'I'll clear up here.'

'Are you sure? I was hoping we might…'

'Jack, what with your dodgy leg and the size of your shower cubicle, you're not going to be able to lift any more than a bar of soap. Anyway, I had a shower before I came over. Do it now, before this Merlot wears off.'

'Okay, I'll be quick. As quick as I can, anyway.'

'What are you doing?' she asked as he took a supermarket *Bag for Life* from the kitchen.

'It's to wrap around my leg,' he explained. 'To keep the wound as dry as I can.'

She laughed. 'I'll be ready when you come out.'

He sat on the edge of his bed and slowly undressed. He was getting used to the injury, and it did not seem to be as painful as earlier, although that could be the painkillers working. He wrapped the bag around the top of his leg and got in the shower. He found it easier than he expected, and his makeshift leg shroud seemed to work fairly well; the fact that his leg was sheltered by his upper body helped.

He felt better after the shower, cleaner and fresher. He returned to his bedroom and lay down on the bed. Susan followed him in and laughed.

'What's the matter?' he asked.

'Jack, you look really sexy wearing nothing but a carrier bag.'

'Oh, yes.'

He sat up to untie it.

'Leave it. I'll do it,' she said softly as she took off her top. Seconds later she was naked. She sat on the edge of the bed and gently untied the bag. She looked at his wound, leaned down and gently kissed it.

'Thank you, nurse,' Jack whispered.

She climbed onto the bed, on all fours astride him, kissing around the wound again. 'Mustn't get it wet,' she grinned as she slowly made her way to the top of his leg and around his stomach.

'I don't want to peak too early,' Jack said quietly, running his hand through her hair. She looked him in the eyes and raised herself over him, reaching back to position him inside her. Jack exhaled loudly as she began to rock.

'You okay?' she asked, brushing her hand across his injured leg.

'More than okay. What are you doing?' he asked as she paused and leaned over to the side of the bed.

She picked up her phone, and found the camera app.

CHAPTER TWENTY-FOUR

Levi lay on his bed, head propped up on two pillows. He cocked his ears to make sure nobody was hanging around the landing. Not that what he was doing made any noise, but he didn't want any of his housemates bursting into his room and potentially seeing what he was doing.

He had just logged into the *BoyZone* app, and was reading his messages. This was where most of the men he saw got in touch with him. He did use others, but this was the main one. Here he was known as Loki. It would have been obvious that this was an alias, but as long as his anonymity was preserved, he didn't give a shit.

Since he was on the night before, he had had two messages. One he dismissed straightaway: a nineteen year old, apparently, who wanted to negotiate down from the hundred pounds Levi was asking. He responded that he would go down to fifty if the nineteen year old just wanted a blow, but the counter offer was twenty-five. Levi said to forget it, and deleted the messages.

The other message was more promising. He was thirty-eight and straight. He seemed the ideal candidate: he would most likely be partnered or married, probably kids. And plenty to lose.

It was at this point that Levi realised something: there was no Navindra anymore. Nobody to get in place with a good view of where Levi would meet the man. he didn't need to have a full view of the act in question: Levi and the man going into an empty building, or vehicle, that was normally enough. It would be possible to get somebody else, but not at this short notice. He would have to turn the guy down.

Then Levi realised how much money he had left, or didn't have to be precise. It had been over a week since the last trick. From what he could see from the guy's profile and pictures, it should be a pretty easy meet. A hundred quid for ten minutes' work. Maybe this guy would be lucky, and wouldn't get shaken down. This time: if he enjoyed himself enough, then maybe a repeat meeting would be possible, and that could be videoed.

He arranged to meet the client in Limehouse. The client, apparently called William, said he was an electrician, and was doing some work in a house off Limehouse Causeway. The place was being renovated, and was empty, so they could meet there. Levi said okay, and arranged to meet William at the end of the street at nine thirty. At that time, the streets would be quiet.

After he had eaten, Levi showered and cleaned himself up for the rendezvous. The guy wanted full sex, so Levi had to be ready for that; he also insisted on safe sex: that was good, as it meant that the guy was not single. Even though it wouldn't be tonight, Levi would make sure the guy left happy, wanting another encounter.

The meeting place was around the corner from the Westferry Docklands Light Railway station. Again, an easy meet for Levi: he could service the guy, take his hundred, and be on his way home within half an hour.

Nine twenty-six and he was turning into Limehouse Causeway. On the corner, looking in a shop window was a middle-aged man, short hair and a beard, wearing a white hoodie, which William said he would be wearing.

'Hey,' Levi said as he approached. 'You

William?'

'William,' the man acknowledged. He seemed nervous; an ideal customer. 'You okay?'

'I'm good.'

'It's this way,' William said, indicating they should go further down the street. As they walked, William said, 'There's just a couple of things that have cropped up.'

'Oh yes?' Levi asked. This was quite normal, clients asking for a reduction at the last minute.

'The owner of the house I'm working in has come home unexpectedly, so we can't use there.'

'Anywhere else we could go?' Levi asked. There were plenty of dark places here.

'My van's parked around the corner. We could use that, if you'd be up for that.'

'Do it in your van? Yeah, no problem.' It wouldn't have been the first time.

'The other thing is, could my workmate join in? If you say no, that's cool: he can just piss off for a walk for half an hour. He'll pay the same as me.'

Levi hadn't expected this, but the thought of two hundred pounds for thirty minutes' work was irresistible.

'That's no problem.'

'Great,' said William, excitedly. 'We could go one each end, then swap over.'

They turned a corner, and parked around this

corner was a white van. William's workmate stood leaning on the van: in the darkness, Levi could only make out a silhouette. As they approached, the man pushed himself off the side of the van.

'This is Harry,' William said. 'Harry, this is Loki. He's cool about having the two of us.'

Harry nodded at Levi. 'Hi. Do we pay you now?'

'If you don't mind.'

'No problem,' Harry said, and got out his wallet. Gave Levi five twenties. William did the same, only a mix of twenties and tens, plus two fives.

William unlocked the back of the van. 'There's a light inside,' he explained, 'but I won't switch it on until we're inside. Just in case we attract attention.' He used the torch function on his phone to unlock the rear doors and to jump in first. Levi could make out William standing in the centre of the van, and shelves of stuff on one side.

Harry put a hand on Levi's shoulder. 'After you, Levi,' he said.

Levi lifted a foot to the van step, then turned. The back of his neck suddenly felt cold and clammy.

'Hey, how do you -'

CHAPTER TWENTY-FIVE

Jack saw Susan off at just after ten, waving her goodbye as her taxi disappeared around the corner. He shivered as he turned and went back inside. He hurried as it was drizzling and it was cold, his haste serving to exaggerate his limp. He was wearing a sweat shirt and pants and a pair of trainers. She had told him to put on a coat if he was going outside but he brushed this off. Maybe she was right.

Back inside, he flopped back down onto the bed. The bed was still untidy. He kicked off his trainers and picked up his phone. Susan had sent him a couple of WhatsApp messages with the footage from an hour or so earlier. He propped himself up on a pillow and viewed them again, nodding in approval. He felt a twinge in his leg. He had probably overexerted himself: he had intended to keep his legs prone on the bed and let her do the work, but that did not happen.

He decided it was time for another painkiller, and padded into the kitchen and brewed a cup of tea with which to take the tablet.

Back on the bed, he saw that she had messaged that she had got home safely and she hoped his leg would get better soon, as that evening probably hadn't helped! He sent laughing, thumbs up and kiss emojis and said he would speak to her soon.

Then he noticed another message which had come through a minute ago. It was from Levi.

Hey u free?

Jack replied, **Not tonight. Why? You got more to tell me?**

Can we meet up sometime soon?

Can do. What about same time and place as before?

There was a pause.

2 far.

It wasn't too far before, Jack thought. **What do you want to tell me? You want to earn some more money?** He paused a bit before adding, **Wasn't £75 enough?**

Want sum more. Got more things 2 tell u.

Okay, Jack replied. **Where do you want to meet?**

U know Limehouse?

Sort of. Where in Limehouse? When? Tomorrow morning?

How about corner of Limehouse causeway and Gill Street?

OK, Jack typed reluctantly. **What time?**

U cant make 2nite?

No. has to be tomorrow.

Wot about 9pm?

Shit, he thought. He didn't really want to go all the way down to Limehouse at that time. It looked like he had no choice. He typed his agreement.

Cool, came the response.

Jack waited a minute or so: there were no other messages so he assumed the conversation was over. He was a bit puzzled: Paddington wasn't too far for Levi before; in fact, they met there at his suggestion. Then, it was strange that Levi had forgotten how much Jack had paid him.

Jack frowned. There was something odd here.

The next morning, Jack's leg was sore. Time for more painkillers. He had definitely overdone it the night before.

After breakfast, he sat at his little desk, and opened up his laptop and notepad. His phone pinged: it was a text from Cathy.

Morning, Dad. How is your leg? Are you taking it easy?

Getting there. Taking it easy, yes. Two lies in one message.

Cool. CU Friday?

See you Friday x

He took a large gulp of black coffee and began to flesh out the structure of his article. His first port of call would be social media. He started with Jaylon and Facebook. There were two entries for his name, one in Thodupuzha, India, and the other in Al Ajman, wherever the hell that was. This was not surprising. He also checked on Instagram, and found nothing. There was no point looking anywhere else, so he turned his attention to the victim.

Navindra Dhabi had a much higher social media presence. There was one living in Kuwait, another in Leicester, and two in London. The one Jack was seeking had his face on his profile.

Success, he thought at first, but there were few postings, mainly obscure pictures or gifs, most of which were obscene in some way. Jack's mother always said there was nothing more uninteresting than looking at other people's holiday photographs: Jack updated that to other people's Facebook postings. Navindra had a couple of dozen friends, all with a similar age and ethnic background. He was hoping for a face he recognised: maybe Levi, maybe the two who confronted him; but there was nothing.

He continued looking, but it was beginning to feel intrusive.

Earlier that morning, Albert (Albie) Cooper was taking Shane, his four year-old husky, for a pre-breakfast walk. Albie and Shane took their usual route: out of the flat in Dod Street, making a right along Burdett Road, then stopping off at the convenience store for the *Daily Mirror*. They would walk as far as the bridge over the Limehouse Cut, then down the steps to the path which ran alongside the canal. They would take the path as far as the next bridge, then up the steps to the street. The Cut would continue to Bromley, where it would merge with the River Lea, which would then meander north.

Back on the street, Albie and Shane would make a circuit of the streets, ending up at Bartlett Park, where Shane would have the chance to cock and squat. Then it was back home for breakfast.

Today would be slightly different. As Albie

and Shane made their way along the path, they came across another dog walker, which was not uncommon, who had two Frenchies on leads. Albie saw the woman quite frequently, and they would exchange greetings as they passed. Today, she was standing still, the dogs straining at the leash, and looking out at the canal.

'It's too cold for a swim!' Albie called out as he and Shane approached. The woman didn't seem to appreciate the joke; instead she kept staring at the water, jabbing her finger.

Albie paused, letting Shane and one of the Frenchies touch noses. 'You seen a body or something?'

She was pointing at something in the water. As the current brought the object closer, Albie could see what it was.

She stopped pointing, but put her hand to her mouth. 'Oh, my God! Oh, my God!'

CHAPTER TWENTY-SIX

EARLY THAT EVENING, Jack set off for Limehouse. He planned on getting there long before nine. He was on the last stage of his journey: the Docklands Light Railway. During the afternoon, he tried driving round the block a few times, but felt it was too soon to attempt a longer drive. Maybe in a few days.

This had better be worth it, he thought. Even without a painful leg, it was a long tube journey to Caledonian Road, then Shadwell, down to Westferry, which involved walking and stairs at every change. There was no way he was going to use the lifts; that was for old people.

Whilst he sat on the train, like almost every other passenger, he began to surf his phone. Eventually, he came across BBC News, where one piece stood out. An unidentified body had been found, that of a young male adult, in the Limehouse Cut. The body was found that morning by two dog walkers. The person had no identification on him, empty pockets in fact, but appeared to be of Middle Eastern descent. He was wearing a blue denim jacket, black combat-style trousers, and black and white trainers. Cause of death was yet to be determined.

Jack sat bolt upright, staring out of the window opposite. Yesterday, Levi was wearing a blue denim jacket. He couldn't be so sure about the rest of what he was wearing, but definitely the jacket. He was in his twenties, of Middle Eastern background, maybe; definitely not Caucasian.

Limehouse Cut was not a million miles from where he said to meet Jack. Things were starting to fit into place. If that was Levi in the Cut, then who texted Jack last night? Whoever it was, had no idea how much Jack had paid. He needed to think through what he needed to do; there was no way he was going to end up in the canal too.

It had to be Levi. The age, the ethnicity.

The blue denim jacket.

More than a coincidence.

The report said no cause of death had been

established, but Jack was certain it wasn't drowning.

Not accidental drowning, anyway.

Jack had a big question: assuming Levi's death was related to their meeting at Paddington, how did anybody else know? More immediately, who the hell was Jack on his way to meet? Jack didn't believe in coincidences: if Levi was killed to silence him, was the same thing planned for Jack?

He debated going to the police; but in reality, what could he add to their investigation? They didn't have Levi's phone, so would have no knowledge of their conversations.

A thought passed through his head briefly. What if it was the police messaging him, pretending to be Levi as part of their investigation? He dismissed that thought immediately: there was no way the police would arrange to meet him in a quiet street in Limehouse at nine o'clock at night.

Tragic as it was, Levi's death did confirm one thing: that Jack was on the right track. Levi was silenced because of something he had told Jack, or something his killers thought he had told him.

He read the article one more time. He was almost there. One more stop. He would need to work out what to do next with regard to his investigation; in the short term, he needed to be on his guard now.

Ironically, the meeting location was not far from Jack's office. As the crow flies, that is. The meeting was scheduled for nine PM. It was ten past eight when he arrived. He walked along Limehouse Causeway, walking with a purpose, not aimlessly like somebody about to meet another. He passed the junction of the Causeway and Gill Street, where the meeting was scheduled to take place. The dark streets were deserted. No pedestrians, just a few cars parked here and there.

He walked as far as a small park, Ropemakers Field. He sat on a bench, and started to work out what to do. He always made a point of getting to a meeting location early, especially in situations such as this. He needed a secure and hidden vantage point from where he could observe the meeting point. He had passed a school: maybe that would serve.

He walked around the block a couple of times, just to familiarise himself with the locale. Across the road from Gill Street was the school, and next to the school was an empty building, which contained offices. Jack found that if he stood in the doorway of the office building, he was concealed by the doorway and the school railings. Maybe not during the day, but definitely at night.

At 8:43, a white van pulled up, parking on the Causeway, three or four cars' length from the junction. Two men got out. They looked around, then both checked their phones. One lit up a cigarette, and the other walked over to the junction. Jack stepped further back in the doorway. He was satisfied he could not be seen. There was a street lamp at the junction; where Jack was, was in darkness.

He had no doubt: the white van was meant for him, as it had been for Levi before.

It was now five minutes to nine. The man standing on the corner walked back to his colleague. They had a brief conversation, then the second went to stand behind the van – hidden – while the first returned to the street corner. The one behind the van lit another cigarette.

Jack texted Levi's number: **Sorry, running a bit late. At Shadwell. Be 10-15.**

Jack could see the man on the corner check his phone.

Then Jack's pinged. 'Shit!' he whispered, desperately silencing it. In the silent streets, the ping sounded loud, but fortunately a car was passing by. The one hiding behind the van seemed not to have heard anything. Jack checked the message. **No worries, I'll be here.**

Jack looked over at them again. They were still there, waiting. Waiting for him. They had no idea he was there, but he didn't need to be here anymore. Two against one was not good odds at the best of times, but two, possibly with weapons, against one with a dodgy leg: well, they were even worse odds. Especially as the leg was beginning to ache again.

The one behind the van lit yet another cigarette, and while he was distracted, Jack quickly stepped out of the doorway, and headed down the street, keeping as close to the building as he could. A few yards further on was a cul-de-sac, short and comprising half a dozen mews houses. Jack paused once he had rounded the corner, straightened his clothing, and walked again with a purpose, out of the mews, turning left and walking to the next junction. He did not look round.

The road he was in now was called Three Colt Street, where he had checked earlier. He carried on walking, in effect walking in a circle, on his way back to the station.

CHAPTER TWENTY-SEVEN

JACK STOPPED. HE was about a hundred yards from the station.

'To hell with this,' he said aloud, before turning on his heels and walking back. Back to the doorway. Again, he walked with a purpose, only slowing down when he got to the corner of Limehouse Causeway. As before, he walked as close to the wall, as much in the darkness as he could.

They were still there. One figure behind the van, the other on the corner. He noticed a text had arrived while he was walking back.

Where ru?

Jack replied: **You will have to get up earlier in the morning to get one up on me.**

The guy on the corner, who clearly had Levi's phone, read the message and looked around. Then he walked quickly back to the other one. Jack could just about make out them both looking at the phone. Then another message came through.

WTF? U here yet?

Jack replied: **Fuck you.**

Then his phone rang. Even though he had it switched to silent, the vibration still made a sound. Jack squeezed his pocket to muffle the sound. Fortunately, an aircraft was flying above, either on its way to, or on its way from, the City Airport, and that camouflaged the sound. Once the vibration had stopped, Jack checked the phone. A missed call from Levi's number.

He waited, watching. Waiting to see what they would do.

After a minute or so, the guy with Levi's phone walked back to the van, said something to the other, and they both got into the van, which pulled away.

Jack waited a minute, then took a deep breath and began to walk back to the station. It was time to go home. He had had some fun with them, although that had not served any useful purpose. He just had to decide what to do next.

Two cars passed him as he walked back, and a

couple, arms linked, walked in the other direction the other side of the road. Then another vehicle passed him, his side of the road. He was aware that the sound of that vehicle's engine was slightly different to that of a car, but as it passed he realised that it was the white van. The speed limit on this street was twenty miles per hour. The cars were probably travelling at that speed, but the van was going much more slowly, fifteen, or even ten. They had to be checking the streets. As it slowly overtook him, Jack forced himself to look straight ahead, avoid any eye contact. There was no reason for the men in the van to know what he looked like, so he just had to remain cool.

By the time he reached the station, the van had passed and continued around the bend in the road. Jack hurried up the steps to the station; at the top he looked back at the empty street.

His heart was racing.

Next morning, Jack took a painkiller with a cup of coffee. It occurred to him then that he had very little trouble with the leg the night before: as he was hurrying back to the station, he could not recall limping. He shrugged: maybe it was the adrenalin. While he was on the train back home he received messages from both Cathy and Susan asking how his leg was. In both cases, he replied that it was okay, and that he was taking it easy. Thank God they were both messages, not video calls.

He sat down with his open laptop. He needed to find out more about Navindra Dhabi. He had already looked at his social media presence, which had not helped much. Did he work? The neighbours had told Jack that he was often loitering around the estate, but did he have a job? Jack had only been assigned to the trial; he did not recall anything about the murder itself when it happened. The murder would have been in the news at the time; it was just that Jack did not cover it himself.

He logged into the *Daily News* archive and looked. Eventually he found something. Three lines, no more. Sadly, the stabbing of a twenty-something in the middle of a gang fight was hardly front page news.

He tried the *Standard* archive section. Again, just three or four lines, relating the news, but this time there was a quotation about him. It was from somebody called Simon Ray from Spitalfields Radio. The quotation was brief, and that, "a young man with so much potential had been taken from us way too soon."

Jack was not sure he had heard of Spitalfields

Radio, so Googled them. It was as it said on the tin: a local radio station based in Spitalfields, a small district of East London sandwiched between Whitechapel and Shoreditch. The station's website proclaimed it as a not for profit organisation for East London, which welcomed donations. There was even a little yellow DONATE button. Credit cards and direct debit were welcome, too.

The station was based in Commercial Street, which was the main thoroughfare which ran through the district. Just on the District and Hammersmith & City lines, so a relatively easy place to get to. Jack considered just picking up the phone, but experience had taught him that whilst it was easy to refuse to answer any questions and hang up the phone, it was not so easy face to face. So he set off for Spitalfields.

On his way there, for want of anything better to do, Jack did some research on the location. The name first appeared in 1399 as *Spittellond*, and over the centuries became what it is today. *Spital* is a corruption of the word hospital: the land once belonged to St Mary Spital, a priory or hospital for travellers run by a religious order. It became an autonomous area, or hamlet, of the parish of Stepney in the eighteenth century, and was incorporated into the County of London towards the end of the nineteenth. It is formed around

Commercial Street, and includes the area around Christ Church, Toynbee Hall, and Brick Lane. It is also home to several markets, including Petticoat Lane Market and Spitalfields Market.

And also Spitalfields Radio.

The locale had changed very little since the production of Google Streetview, and Jack was easily able to find the radio station. Two minutes' walk from Aldgate East, in a small parade of commercial premises, sandwiched between former bank premises, now a wine bar, and a nail salon. Jack went in. A girl with bright red hair was sitting at a reception desk, playing with her mobile phone. Music was playing over a loudspeaker: Jack assumed it was what the station was broadcasting at the time, and this was confirmed when a voice announced what the music was and began talking about an event at Spitalfields Market that weekend.

'Can I help you?' the girl asked. She had a local accent and spoke as if Jack was interrupting whatever she was doing.

'Yes,' said Jack, leaning on the counter. 'I'd like to speak to Simon Ray.'

'No-one here with that name,' she said.

'There must be, or must have been; he was quoted in the paper.'

She looked at Jack, stood up and went to the door that was behind her. Opening the door a few inches, she said, 'Scott? Do you know someone called Simon Ray? Man outside says he works here.' She came back in, said, 'He's coming,' to Jack, then sat down again.

A man appeared at the door: late twenties, tall and bulky, black hair slicked back. 'You're asking about Simon?' he asked, stepping towards Jack.

'Yes, I wanted to talk to him about something.'

'And you are?'

Jack fished out a business card and handed it to Scott. 'Simon spoke to us about something a few months back, and we're doing a follow-up piece, so I needed to talk to him some more.'

'Oh, I'm sorry,' said Scott as he handed the card back, 'but Simon doesn't work here anymore.'

'Oh, no,' said Jack. 'Where is he now?'

'He left broadcasting in the summer. Works for a newspaper now. Small world,' Scott laughed.

'Really? Which one?'

'Oh, nothing like yours. It's called...' Scott paused a second while he recalled. '*Attitude*. That's it: *Attitude*.'

'*Attitude*,' Jack repeated, to confirm.

'Yeah. It's an LGBT paper, not mainstream.'

'Where are they based, do you know?'

'I can't remember exactly. We met up for a

beer a while after he left. A pub in Highbury. I think it's near there. Sorry, I can't be any more help.'

'No worries. Thanks for your time,' Jack said as he left. Back on the street, he Googled *Attitude*. As Scott had said, it was a niche publication for the lesbian, gay, bisexual and transgender community, and was based on Seven Sisters Road, just up from Finsbury Park. 'Finsbury Park, then,' he said resignedly and headed back down the road.

He was soon in Seven Sisters Road, and started to walk away from the park and down to the *Attitude* offices. He recalled the last time he was here: some years ago he was investigating people trafficking, and he was entertained by an elderly sex worker in her flat just up the road. His recollection was that he gave her some cash, though for information only, not for any services.

He found the premises, just after the fork in the road. He actually walked past it at first, thinking it was an empty unit. The door and window frames were blackened, and one of the shopfront windows and part of the door were boarded over. He tried the door, but it was locked. Inside, he could see a light, and thought he could make out a figure on the premises. He knocked on the door. The figure looked up and walked over to the door. He fiddled with a key, and opened the door.

'Yes? Can I help you?'

'I'm looking for Simon Ray,' Jack said, holding up one of his cards. 'Scott over at Spitalfields Radio sent me over.'

'Oh, did he now?' the man said. 'I'm Simon. Do you want to come in?'

'Thanks.' Jack stepped inside. Simon locked the door behind them.

'Come this way,' Simon said. 'Sorry about the mess. We were firebombed at the weekend.'

CHAPTER TWENTY-EIGHT

HE LED JACK out to a small office at the back, through what remained of an outer office: a desk, a chair which was standing at an angle as one leg was missing. A couple of metal filing cabinets, one where its shape had been distorted. On the desk was a screen, which had almost melted. Only the stand and the frame of the screen remained. The furniture was black, as were the walls to the front of the premises. Blackened, burnt sheets of paper lay strewn all over the floor, on which there were numerous puddles of water.

'When did all this happen, then?' Jack asked, as they walked through.

Ray turned and offered Jack a chair in the untouched room. 'Saturday evening,' he said. 'It was about seven. Dark. Fortunately, I was on the premises. I was working at the desk and had come out here to make myself a cup of tea, when someone pushed... it was like a coke bottle filled with paraffin or something, lighted rag stuffed in the top, and... well, you can see what happened.'

'Jesus,' Jack said, turning to look at the damage.

'Quite. It's not the first time it's happened. That's why I always kept an extinguisher and fire blanket near the door; but this time, it was too much. There's a fire station a mile or so away, so they were here quite quickly. It could have been a lot worse. Probably the water's done more damage than the fire or the smoke.'

'They say that, yes. And this is all because of what?'

'Because of the type of magazine we publish. Simple as that. You would have thought that almost in the second quarter of the twenty-first century, that sort of bigotry would be a thing of the past, but I'm afraid it's very much with us. Very much.'

'I'm afraid human nature never changes,' Jack said sadly.

There was a pause, then Ray said, 'You wanted to ask me about Navindra Dhabi.'

'Yes, I do. How did you know?'

'I had a feeling. Why the interest in him?'

'The trial of the boy they arrested for Navindra's murder was scheduled to begin last week.'

'Really? I didn't know that. You said *was*.'

'The accused, Jaylon Soji, changed his plea to guilty at the last minute. So no trial.'

'He's been sentenced?'

'Not as yet. The judge adjourned for reports. Do you know Jaylon Soji? There looked like a flash of recognition on your face.'

'No. No, I don't know him. Maybe I recalled the name from when he was arrested. So: Navindra.'

'I was assigned to cover the trial -'

'Which isn't happening now.'

'But there will be some public interest when sentence is passed; so I'm looking to write a piece about the victim. A kind of human interest thing, you know? I took a look at the archives from when the murder took place, and saw a quotation or two from yourself, suggesting you knew him.'

'So you contacted the radio station and they sent you here?'

'Pretty much. You knew him, then?'

'That was a mistake giving that quote; I should have kept my mouth shut.'

'You didn't know him?'

'I was quite cut up when I heard the news about his death. Hence my quote. I thought at the time it wasn't the best idea, association with him and all that. But I thought what the hell?'

'You've lost me.'

'I knew him, sort of. We kind of did business together. This isn't going into your paper, is it?'

'I just need some background stuff on him, not you.'

'I'll trust you. One journalist to another, professional courtesy, you might say. I used to buy stuff from him.'

'Drugs?'

Ray nodded. 'Cocaine, now and again. Poppers, a bit more frequently.'

'How did you do that? Meet him, I mean.'

'He and another boy, they used to pose as homeless guys, outside the supermarkets, you know?'

Jack nodded. 'They're almost invisible.'

'They'd be lying or sitting there, in their sleeping bags. Plastic cup or something in front of them. I'd walk past, pretend to drop a fiver or something in their cup. It'd be more, of course: a lot more. I wasn't his only customer, of course; for anything. Then we'd meet somewhere – sometimes at mine if we were minded to do anything – and he'd hand over the shit there.'

'Why didn't you pay him then? Why the charade at the supermarket?'

'He needed the cash first to get from his supplier. And he couldn't have the stuff on him then in case he got picked up.'

'You trusted him to bring the coke?'

'I had no choice. In any case, if we did anything else, he'd get paid for that too. At least a hundred.'

'Anything else?'

Ray gave Jack a stare which said it all.

It clicked. 'I get you,' Jack said. 'So,' he went on, 'that's how it all worked. Cash at the supermarket, and the drugs later at your place.'

'Why are you so interested in that? I thought you just wanted some personal stuff about Navindra.'

'I do, sorry. Tell me what you know about him.'

'Not much. Just like I told you. We never chatted much; it was just business. I think he lived with his family. Mother, father, siblings – I don't know how many or what they were. I think he let it slip once that he was nineteen. Short, slight build. Nice arse.' He sniggered. 'Always clean, smelt good. But then he'd have to be if he wanted an extra hundred.'

'How often did you see him? For business, I mean.'

'Once a month, something like that. Once I'd used up my supply, I'd text him, and we'd arrange a pick up for the cash. Then I'd generally meet him at mine.' Ray was beginning to loosen up, Jack felt. 'He came round with a boyfriend once.'

'A boyfriend?'

'I didn't mean boyfriend in that sense. We'd agreed a time for him to come over with some coke, agreed we'd have some fun as well, and he asked if I was up for a threesome. I'd have to pay extra, of course; but that wasn't a problem.'

'Tell me about the boyfriend.'

Ray shrugged. 'Same as him, really. Same age. Navindra told me once his family were Sri Lankan. I'm not sure if his friend was, but he wasn't white. I don't mean he was black, just not Caucasian. Sort of Asian, maybe Sri Lankan as well. Did that sound racist? I didn't mean…'

'I get the picture. Go on.'

'He was similar age, similar build, as well. He told me his name; what was it?' Ray paused a second, then clicked his fingers. 'Loki. That was it.'

'Loki? As in… Thor?'

'That's it. Obviously not his real name, but I didn't give a shit.'

Jack had a feeling. 'Can you remember what he was wearing?' he asked.

'What he was wearing? No. Nothing out of the ordinary. He was naked most of the time.'

'When they arrived, was this Loki wearing a denim jacket? A blue denim jacket?'

Ray looked Jack in the eye. 'Yes, I think he was. Why? Do you know him?'

Jack nodded.

'I did. He's dead as well now.'

CHAPTER TWENTY-NINE

THE SUPERMARKET IN question was the large Tesco Extra on Morning Lane, in Hackney.

One of the last things Simon Ray said before he showed Jack out was, 'They won't look like a normal homeless person. That's how you tell.' When Jack looked round for an explanation, all Ray did was tap the side of his nose and close the door to the premises.

'Bloody mind games,' Jack muttered, and headed back to the tube station.

The supermarket was five minutes' walk from Hackney station, so was a relatively easy journey for Jack; even his leg seemed to be getting better.

It was now just after two: that time of year, dusk was at six-thirty, so he had at least three hours of usable daylight left.

From the pavement, there was a path leading through the large car park to the store entrance, a mixture of zebra crossing and tactile paving. It was a pain not having the car, he reflected: it would have made the next few hours a bit more bearable. He couldn't afford to wait, though, until he could drive again.

The supermarket was fronted by a sort of patio, under a glass canopy. Rows and rows or trolleys of varying sizes and capacities. Three ATMs. On the left, large glass sliding doors leading inside. Between the doors and the row of ATMs was a figure sitting against the wall, the lower half of his body nestled inside a sleeping bag. Jack slowed down as he walked past this figure into the supermarket, casually glancing down at him. He looked no different to the dozens of others he saw on the streets.

There was nothing he needed to buy here; in any case, while he had the daylight, he wanted to watch the man. The supermarket café was near the entrance, and he was able to find a table for two in the window, where he had a clear view of the figure in the sleeping bag. He put his coffee on the table and waited, checking things on his phone to avoid looking suspicious. He had already taken a free newspaper from the stand in the entrance and occasionally glanced at that.

As he waited, he discretely looked the man over to see what was different about him. He could identify nothing: what was Ray talking about, unless this was a genuine person? He had a plastic beaker standing in front of him; occasionally a passer-by would lean down to drop a coin in; the man would make brief eye contact before resuming staring into space.

Jack decided to take a closer look. He had finished his coffee by now, and walked out to the front of the store. One of the ATMs - the one closest to the man – was out of use, and there was a short queue of two or three people at the remaining two. As he waited, he surreptitiously studied the man, but could see nothing different. He was maybe early thirties, long hair, beard. He was smoking a rolled up cigarette. What was inside the cigarette paper, however, was anybody's guess.

It was Jack's turn. Still keeping the man in view of the corner of his eye, he slid in his bank card, checked his balance and withdrew two hundred pounds. He had had to give Simon Ray fifty for his information, so needed cash on him anyway. He just had to remember to claim the money back at the end of the week.

As Jack put his wallet back into his pocket,

and turned to vacate the space in front of the ATM, he was aware of the man getting out of his sleeping bag and standing up. Jack could see he was wearing a red and black puffer jacket, which looked surprisingly clean. Corduroy trousers and black trainers. Jack walked over to the edge of the patio and leaned on one of the concrete bollards while he pretended to take a phone call.

A second man had approached the guy in the puffer jacket. Around the same age, he was wearing a thick grey fleece. His hair was jet black, whereas the others was auburn. He also sported a black beard and his hair was tied severely back into a small ponytail at the top of the back of his head.

The two men exchanged a bro hug and swapped places, the one in the puffer jacket tipping the contents of the beaker into his left pocket. As the second man sat down and slipped into the sleeping bag, the first walked past Jack, making no eye contact, over to the crossing. Still on his fictitious phone call, Jack followed the man, who seemed to be heading for the main road.

The pedestrian crossing lights were green as the man crossed. Having ended his phone call, Jack hurried across after him as the lights began counting down: 4-3-2…

It seemed they were both headed for the bus

stop. Jack's quarry stepped into the shelter with three other passengers; Jack hung around discretely with two others, one of whom was smoking a cigarette.

A bus arrived, a single decker, number 394. The man stepped into the line to get onto the bus; Jack did the same. As Jack boarded, he could see the man heading for a seat near the back. He took one four rows from the front, so would see when the man got off. The bus's final destination was Islington, and as it made its way, Jack checked online its exact route: none of the stops seemed particularly important, so where was he headed? Maybe he was just going home.

Then something clicked. Jack was considering how he could have afforded a new puffer jacket, assuming it wasn't stolen, but that wasn't all: he recalled the man's fingers. They were neatly cut and clean. His hair was down to his shoulders, was washed. Shiny, in fact. His teeth, what Jack saw of them, were well-maintained and white. The sleeping bag, for that matter, bore none of the dirt and wear which one would have expected. So that was what Simon Ray had been talking about. This man was the exact antithesis of what one would have expected in a person sleeping rough. The one who appeared to relieve him was the same. In London, people sleeping rough are so ubiquitous they are practically invisible. Hiding in plain sight.

About half an hour later, Jack was aware of the bell pinging and the *Bus Stopping* light illuminating. He stirred as he saw the man pass him as he walked to the front of the bus, standing behind two other passengers. Jack looked out of the window: they were approaching Angel. Four hundred years earlier, there was a pub here on the corner of Pentonville Road and Islington High Street called the *Angel Inn*, which over time lent its name to the entire area.

As Jack also got off the bus, he could see the man waiting to cross Pentonville Road. Jack did the same, staying a few yards behind, and making sure there were two or three people between them. Once across the road, the man began to walk up the High Street, turning left into Liverpool Road. He was walking quite quickly, and Jack had to quicken his pace to avoid losing him. His leg was beginning to get sore; fortunately he had brought his painkillers with him, and so was able to swallow two as he followed the man up the road, past the Waitrose supermarket and into the residential part of Islington.

From East London to here, Jack thought, what the hell is going on?

CHAPTER THIRTY

JACK WONDERED IF the man was headed to Angel tube station, but he stayed on the same side of the road, turning left up Liverpool Road, just opposite the tube. Where did this road lead, he wondered. He tried to visualise a London street map, but all he could come up with was that this road went north, and into Islington, then Barnsbury.

He was walking briskly, and Jack had to quicken his own pace to keep up. With luck, his leg would hold out.

He paused a second outside the Waitrose supermarket, and Jack did the same, expecting to have to follow him around there. Ironic, he thought, to go in here after he had spent so long outside another supermarket. A cheaper one, Jack thought.

But no, after a few seconds' pause, he went on, still at a brisk pace.

They had probably walked about two hundred yards, when they came to a parade of around a dozen shops. One of these was a convenience store, and the man walked in there. Jack followed, a few yards behind.

Inside the store, there were three aisles of shelves, each going back about a hundred feet. The door matched up with the centre aisle, and to the right of the door, against the front wall, was the counter, with two tills. The counter seemed to be on a slightly raised platform. A man was behind one of the tills, serving a woman. He seemed early thirties, long straggly beard, with hair tied back. Jack guessed he was South Asian. Although he was serving the woman, he was having a loud conversation with somebody else in the shop, whose voice was coming from the far right corner. It was not a language Jack recognised.

Acting out searching the shelves, Jack made his way down the centre aisle. He heard the doorbell ringing a couple of times, signifying people coming into or leaving the store. Then

Jack heard footsteps, as the man hurried up a wooden staircase. Jack went to the back end of the aisle, and was able to get round to where the steps were. At the corner of the store, was a door, leading to a flight of stairs. There was very little room here, and he carefully manoeuvred himself past a woman who was searching though the chilled foods cabinet.

The door remained open, and he took two steps over the threshold, glancing back at the counter. The till was quite busy, with at least two people visible. At least the cashier was occupied.

Jack could hear sounds from upstairs. There was music playing – nothing he recognised: maybe not even Western music. He could hear talking, mixed with some laughter. Male voices, but as before, not in English. He slowly took two steps up to try and hear better. The stairs creaked as he did this: he immediately froze, but there was no reaction from upstairs.

There was no way he was going to risk going further up; he was also concerned that the cashier might be wondering where he had gone, and come to investigate.

Jack remained frozen to the spot, concentrating on what he could hear, but there were no words he could recognise. Until he heard the word *caio*. An Italian word, but understood the world over. Goodbye.

In one long step, he went back downstairs, and nonchalantly walked around the end of the aisle, to where he had been before. Two teenage girls were checking out the cans of soft drinks; Jack made the pretence of studying the canned soups.

He heard footsteps come down the stairs, and walk along the end aisle. He heard some words spoken in the unknown language; then the cashier said, 'Take it easy, Tony.'

Jack looked up the aisle at the door, and saw who it was leaving the store. It was the man he had followed from the Tesco store.

Tony.

He hurried along the aisle, squeezing past the teenagers, trying hard not to touch them. They made no effort to move out of his way. The cashier was involved in taking a large parcel for collection by a courier company, so Jack was able to leave the store unnoticed.

Outside the store, he looked left and right. To the left, he could see Tony walking up Liverpool Road. Dusk was approaching, and the light was fading. He was in danger of losing him.

With Jack in pursuit, Tony crossed over the road and continued his brisk progress along Barnsbury Street. Jack knew this would lead to Upper Street, the other major road leading away from the Angel. Once on Upper Street, Tony made two more turns before appearing to arrive at his destination. He went into a small block of flats, three floors high. Jack could see he went straight in: he must have had a key; there was no speaking into an intercom. So maybe this was where he lived. Home after a heavy day.

Jack gambled on his being there for the foreseeable future, so doubled back to Upper Street, and another convenience store, where he bought himself two Mars bars. He initially took one off the shelf, but took another when he noticed how small the bar was. Is this what they called shrinkflation?

He ate the chocolate and returned to the block of flats, this time noticing the street name: Compton Terrace, N1. He also noticed the block of flats was called Nelson House. Jack wondered if it was named after Nelson Mandela.

Adjacent to the double doors was the inevitable intercom. Twelve buttons, two columns of six. There were no names next to the buttons.

'Here we go,' he said quietly, and pressed button 1. No answer, even after a second time.

Button 2.

'Hello?' a man's voice said.

'Is that Tony?' Jack asked.

'No, pal. Wrong flat.'

This went on until button 5.

'Yeah?' a man's voice came thought the

speaker, sounding younger than flat 2.

'Is that Tony?' Jack asked.

'Who's asking?'

'Tony from the Tesco?'

'Yeah, maybe. Who is this?'

'My name's John. Loki gave me this address.'

'Loki?'

Yeah,' answered Jack. 'Loki.'

'Okay,' said Tony. 'Give me five.'

'No worries,' said Jack, and stepped away from the door. He waited on the pathway to the pavement, stepping to and fro, to keep warm as much as any other reason, regularly checking the time. Nobody entered or left the building while he was waiting.

After six and a half minutes, he heard the lock on the doors click. Jack stepped inside. Flats 1 to 4 were on the ground floor. He walked up to the next floor: flat 5 was immediately at the top of the stairs.

The door was ajar. Jack hesitated, then pushed the door open and went inside.

CHAPTER THIRTY-ONE

PUSHING THE DOOR open, Jack stepped into a narrow hallway. It was carpeted, but the dark carpet was threadbare in some places. There were four doors off the hall, two either side. The first door to the right was open: it was the bathroom. The shower had recently been used, as he could feel the damp and warmth from the bathroom. There was also the scented smell of shower gel in the air.

'I'm in here.' A voice came from behind the door opposite the bathroom. It was half open. The room inside was dark.

Jack closed the flat door, pushed open the

bedroom door and stepped inside. His eyes were getting accustomed to the darkness. A blind was pulled down, but it was only partially opaque, causing the room to be bathed in a half light.

Tony was sitting at the top of the bed, cross-legged. His hair was wet, and he was smoking a rolled-up cigarette. From the smell, Jack could tell it was not ordinary tobacco he was smoking. He was wearing a pair of grey, loose-fitting waffle shorts. His left hand was inside the shorts.

'You're in here,' Jack said as he stepped inside the room.

'Hey, man.' Tony took a drag. 'Who did you say gave you my name? Told you where to find me?'

'He called himself Loki. I doubt if that was his real name.'

'Loki... Loki. I know him: a little guy.'

'Sounds like him,' Jack replied.

'Loki's not his real name.'

'I kind of guessed that,' said Jack, looking around. Apart from the small collapsible table adjacent to the bed, there was minimal furniture here. A wardrobe which must have dated from the sixties, and a wicker chair, across the back of which was a wet towel. An ashtray, a mobile phone, and a pump dispenser rested on the little table.

Tony took a long drag, and rested the cigarette

on the ashtray. 'You going to take your coat off?' he asked.

'I'm good,' said Jack.

'Suit yourself.' Tony lifted himself out of his sitting pose, and walked on his knees across the bed. He reached out for Jack's belt.

Jack took a step back. 'Hey, what are you doing?'

'Isn't that what the little guy sent you here for?'

'No. I want to buy something.'

Tony sat back up. 'I get it. Sorry, I misunderstood.'

'Loki told me I could get some coke from you.'

'Why couldn't he?'

'He didn't offer. I didn't ask.'

'How much are you paying?'

'How much would I get for fifty quid?'

'Fifty would get you a little bag. This size.' With his fingers, Tony indicated a bag around two inches square.

'You got that here?' Jack asked.

Tony shook his head. 'No. You pay me. I get the stuff from my supplier, and pass it over to you.'

'How can I trust you?' Jack asked, taking the cash out of his wallet.

'You know where I live, man.' Tony spoke as

if that answered the question.

Jack tossed two twenties and a ten onto the bed. Tony snatched it up.

'So when do I get the stuff?' Jack asked.

'I'll text you. Give me your number.'

Jack read out his number. He waited until Tony had put it into his phone, then asked, 'Who's your supplier?'

'You don't need to know that, man. It wouldn't be any cheaper buying direct.' He picked up his cigarette and took another long drag.

'Okay,' said Jack. 'How long will it be?'

'A couple of days. Might be tomorrow evening. You interested in some poppers as well?'

'I'm good, thanks.'

'Tomorrow evening, then. Probably.'

Jack said, 'Okay, that'll be good,' as he zipped up his jacket.

Tony walked across the bed again. 'I sell other things as well, you know.' He reached out and began to undo Jack's belt.

'Get the fuck off me,' Jack snapped.

Tony looked into Jack's eyes. 'I'm really good, I promise.'

Jack put his hand on Tony's face, and pushed him back down onto the bed. 'I'm sure you are. You're really high, too.'

Tony sat up and moved back to his position at the top of the bed. His hand went back inside his shorts.

Jack was about to leave, but turned back. 'You want to earn some more cash?'

Tony nodded. 'I'm hungry, man.'

'A hundred?'

Tony nodded, leaning over for another drag.

'I need some information,' Jack said.

'What kind? What about?'

'Where you get the cocaine. Who and where and how. The E8 gang?'

'I don't know what you're talking about. I can't tell you any of that shit.'

Jack laid five twenties at the foot of the bed. 'You sure?'

Tony leaned back, resting his head on the wall. He took a deep breath. 'Fuck.'

Jack looked around for somewhere to sit. He took the wet towel off the chair, tossed it to the far corner of the bed, and sat down.

'Who are you? You the Bill or something?'

Jack explained who he was and what he was doing.

'Not a cop, then?'

'No.'

'I knew that dead kid. He was a friend of Loki's. They used to hang out together.'

'Do you know anything about his murder?'

'Only that he was killed outside where he lived.'

'Is there any word on the streets as to why?'

'Not heard anything. When I heard about it, I supposed it was because of what they were doing.'

'You mean meeting up with men? Is that dangerous, then?'

'That's what I mean. They'd only meet up with certain types of guy, ones with a definite profile. People with families, with partners. Maybe in the public eye, somehow. One of them would meet up with the guy, the other would video it. Maybe set up a camera where they met, or if it was outdoors, be somewhere nearby. Then they'd blackmail him. I assumed one of their punters had got royally pissed off. Why? Isn't that what happened?'

Jack explained about Jaylon. 'You know anything about him? Does the name mean anything?'

Tony kept staring at the cash at the foot of the bed. 'No.'

'Do you do that?' Jack asked, looking around the room. 'Use a camera, I mean. Are we being videoed?'

Tony shook his head, and took a drag. 'I work solo. I just play my part. I sell the coke, or poppers.'

'Or yourself.'

'Or me, that's right. Poppers are cheaper.'

'How do you get the people to buy?'

'If I'm seeing anyone, we get round to talking about it. I say I can get some for fifty quid, and it goes from there. They don't pay me right away. There's a few of us in the gang who pose as beggars outside supermarkets; you know, with the sleeping bags and paper cups?'

'I know.'

'Nobody notices them, or wants to. It's always a bullseye for a bag of the stuff, so they slip it in the cup as they walk past. Easy. So I get the stuff from my fella, then arrange to get it to the punter. Either here, or a room somewhere, or somewhere outdoors, you know?'

Jack deliberately slid the cash a little closer. 'Who is "your fella"?'

'You asking his name?'

Jack sighed. Just tell me where you pick it up. Where it changes hands.'

'This is just between us?'

'Totally. I swear.'

'But your paper…?'

He had made a good point. 'Okay; forget his name, for now. And if I have to write about you, I'll use a different name. Happens all the time.'

'And no police.'

'No police. There's no real evidence, anyway.'

Tony said, 'He operates out of a shop down in Islington, on the main road. Not far from here. The punter passes the money to me like I told you, and I take it to this shop. I pay him, he gives me the bag.'

'How much do you pay?'

Tony clucked; he seemed irritated by this question. 'I pay him thirty for the bag. That's the wholesale price. So yeah, I make twenty on the deal. I hand over the cash, he gives me the package. Not *in* the shop, there's a place upstairs. Then I contact the bloke to arrange delivery.'

'Where in Islington? Can you stop that?'

'Stop what?'

'Stroking yourself. Take your hand out.'

Tony pulled his hand out, used it to pick up the cigarette.

'What's the name of the shop?' Jack asked.

'Don't recall the name. It's one of those 7/11 places, you know? It's next to a slot machine arcade, and some other place. An estate agent, I think.'

'I'll find it,' Jack said. He remembered the slot machine arcade.

'You won't mention me?'

'No, I said I wouldn't.' He took a deep breath. 'I think I've got all I need. Let me know if you think of anything else you can tell me. You know the money's good. I've got your number; I can get hold of you if I need anything else.'

'I'd like that. Maybe we'd have more time.'

'Yeah, maybe,' said Jack sardonically. 'Here,' he said, pushing the twenties to Tony. 'There's your money. Don't spend it all at once, as they say.'

Tony had sat up. He took the money and put it under the ashtray. His hand was down his shorts again. 'You sure there'd nothing else I can give you? Half price?'

'That's very kind of you,' said Jack as he stood up, 'but I just need information. And not a word about me to anyone else, you understand? This is just between us. There might be more where that came from.'

Tony nodded his head.

'I'll let myself out.'

Jack left Tony sitting on his bed, and left the flat and the building. This was all he was going to do tonight. He started to walk back to the Angel; Angel tube was the quickest way home. It was beginning to get dark and cold, and his leg was beginning to throb. After those two Mars bars earlier, he was beginning to get hungry again. Maybe he would stop off nearer home. Or maybe stop for something healthier than chocolate. Some fruit, or something equally unappetising but healthy. Cathy and Susan would be impressed if he did.

As he walked, it occurred to him that Levi, also known as Loki, could well have been murdered as a result of talking to him. He was glad that he had not told Tony that.

CHAPTER THIRTY-TWO

SITTING ON THE train home, Jack noticed that Cathy had tried to call. And texted. Twice.

'Shit,' he muttered. He was so focussed on his visit to Tony that he had forgotten it was Friday, and that his daughter would be going straight from school to his flat. Thank God he had given her a key.

She picked up after one ring.

'Dad! Where are you? I've been worried. You weren't picking up.'

'Sorry, I got tied up here with work. Are you at home?'

'No, I'm at yours. Lucky I had a key.'

'Are you on your way back? Where are you?'

'I've been in Islington. I'm on my way back now, though. I shouldn't be any more than three quarters of an hour.'

'That's good. I can start cooking something. I found some chicken thing in the freezer.'

Jack had no idea what meal she was talking about. 'That'll be great. See you soon.'

He got home just after seven.

'That smells good,' he said, after kissing his daughter.

'Should be ready about seven thirty.'

'Sounds good. Sorry I was late again. You… you didn't call your mother when I didn't answer, did you?' he asked tentatively.

Cathy laughed. 'Of course I didn't. I might have done if you weren't back by now. I might have been worried then.'

'That's my girl,' Jack called out, as he headed to his bedroom to change.

Over dinner, they chatted about how Cathy was doing at school. During this conversation, there were moments of silence. Eventually, Cathy said: 'You're quiet, Dad.'

'Am I? Sorry, I'm just a bit preoccupied with the story I'm working on.' He then related the events of the last few days, just to give her the gist, and missing out some or the more lurid details. She sat there, listening.

'So that's how you hurt your leg?' she eventually asked.

Jack nodded, smiling weakly.

'Why didn't you tell us all this before?'

'It's nothing I can't handle.'

'Even so. Have you told Susan?'

'She knows about the stabbing. That's about it. I told her the other night. Not seen her since.'

'That guy who was murdered: it's not your fault. Susan will tell you that. Even Mum will.'

Jack raised an eyebrow. 'Really? You sure about that?'

Cathy tutted. 'You know what I mean.'

'Yes, I know all that.' Jack put his fork down and pushed the plate away. He had finished eating. 'I'm just telling you how I feel at the moment. It's all still raw. We were chatting down at Paddington, and a few hours later he's floating in Limehouse Basin. Don't worry: I'm sure it will pass.'

'What are you going to do next?'

'I'm going to get some ice cream out of the freezer.'

'Dad…'

'I'm not sure. I think I need to speak to Jaylon again.'

'And Jaylon is…?'

'He's the person all this is about. The kid who was arrested. He's being held in Pentonville, pending reports and sentencing. I keep wondering if he's being a bit economical with the truth, or just not comprehending what's going on.'

'When are you planning on doing that?'

'Monday. I'll do that Monday. Until then, I'm going to put my laptop and notepad away. I'm not even going to talk about work until Monday morning.'

After they had finished eating, they cleared up, and Cathy said she was going into her room to chat with some friends - yes, the ones she was at school with three hours ago – and make a start on her homework.

Jack's leg was beginning to ache: he had taken two painkillers on the way home. They were the non-drowsy type: he hoped they would not keep him awake all night, as there was a lot to do the next day.

He had had a text from Susan while they were eating. She was just checking in to see how he and the leg were and was he free to FaceTime that evening? He messaged her back and said would in half an hour's time be okay, which it was.

He flopped onto his sofa, his aching leg resting on a cushion and began to formulate his next steps in the morning. His first thought was to return to the Islington shop. But to what end? He could hardly say he had been talking to Tony about the drugs they were pushing upstairs, and could he have a quote. He was still no nearer to finding anything about Navindra and why he was murdered, assuming it was not a spontaneous act by Jaylon. All he had begun to establish was that he had been part of the drugs and vice activities of the E8 gang.

And where did that leave Jaylon Soji? He was still found next to the victim's body, covered in the victim's blood, holding the murder weapon.

He decided he needed to talk to Jaylon next. But first he would need to see the boy's mother. But that would have to wait till after the weekend.

Saturday was uneventful, even domestic. Jack and Cathy stayed at home. Cathy alternated between her homework, watching Netflix and chatting, while Jack did his laundry and housework. In the evening, Cathy had arranged to meet friends and go bowling, followed by a trip to Nando's. Jack had arranged the night before that he would call in on Susan as her son was on a sleepover with a classmate. They spent the first hour in bed, then ordered a Chinese meal delivery. Jack picked Cathy up at eleven and they drove back to his flat.

Sunday was a typical Sunday: after sleeping in, Jack drove them into the country for lunch at the Duke of York, a pub in the village of Ganwick Corner. It always amazed Jack the difference a twenty minute drive made; going from city streets with red buses and gridlocked traffic to a bucolic location in no time at all.

After lunch, they went back to Jack's for Cathy to get her stuff, then he took her to her mother's house. Her mother was very matter-of-fact and business-like that afternoon.

'I would chat,' she said dismissively, 'but I've got stuff cooking.'

'No problem,' Jack said. 'I'll head off. See you next week.'

After saying his goodbyes, he headed home, unable to resist a smile at Mel. He knew her well enough to know that she wanted him to ask what she was cooking, and why. Who was she cooking for, to be precise. He felt satisfied that he had wound her up by not showing any interest in her cooking. He knew Cathy would update him in due course, anyway.

CHAPTER THIRTY-THREE

NEXT MORNING HIS leg felt good. It had been twelve hours since he had taken any painkillers. He waited until the rush hour had subsided, then drove the car three or four times around the block. Everything seemed okay. Taking the painkillers with him, he drove down to the Soji house.

As he drove down there, he wondered about calling ahead, but he needed to talk to Mrs Soji, and was almost there anyway.

He managed to find a space eight doors down from the house where the Soji family had their ground floor flat. As he rang the doorbell, he crossed his fingers that she was in; otherwise, this would be a wasted journey, unless he sought out Jaylon's brother.

She was in. Alone, as Jamal was at work. She led him into the kitchen, where, as before, she was at the stove cooking some kind of stew. It smelled good.

'I am surprised to see you, Mr Richardson,' she said. 'How are you getting on? Have you found anything yet to prove my son's innocence? Would you like something to drink? Tea?'

She made him a cup of very milky tea while he replied.

'I'm still working on it. But there's some more information I need either from you, or from Jaylon himself.'

'Go on,' she said, passing him a cup and saucer.

'Somehow, in all of this, two gangs figure: the Kings from here, and the E8, from where the boy was killed. I'm not sure if they were actually rival gangs, but there appears to have been no love lost between them. These gangs keep cropping up. Are you aware of Jaylon having any involvement in gangs?'

'No, no, no. I know all about the gangs. He had nothing to do with them.'

'What about his brother?'

'Jamal has friends, of course. More than

Jaylon does. But no gangs.'

Jack decided not to tell her what Jamal had told him about what went on that night.

'I'd like,' he said, 'to talk to Jaylon again. With your agreement.'

'I was going to go and see him this afternoon.'

'I don't think they'd allow both of us to go. Mrs Soji: can I ask you a favour? Would I be able to go in your place today? I realise it's asking a lot. If you can call the prison and ask if I can go this afternoon instead of you. Tell them I've been before, so they have my details.'

'But then I won't see him till tomorrow.'

'I appreciate that, but it could help to get him released.'

She went silent for a few seconds, then, 'Very well.' She was holding a tea towel which she rested on the table. 'I'll call then now.' She went out into the other room, closing the door behind her. Jack could hear her talking, but could not make out what she was saying. She returned a few minutes later. 'They have agreed. My appointment was at half past three. You can go instead; they said you need to take identification with you.'

'Yes, I know the drill. I appreciate all this, Mrs Soji.' He finished his tea and stood up.

'Can you do me a favour in return?' she asked.

'Of course, anything.'

'Call me later to tell me how he is. And tell him I love him and will see him tomorrow.' She was fighting back tears now. 'And make this visit worthwhile.'

Jack nodded, and left. Before pulling away, he sat silently in the car. He felt so sorry for her.

He started the engine. Time to go back to the prison.

A hundred yards from Mrs Soji's house, Jack pulled over. He had remembered that on his last trip to Pentonville he had gone by tube, and he recalled there was little parking around the prison.

Still in his car, he went online to *JustPark*, an app he had saved as he had used it before, saving himself a lot of time. He made a search of an area with a half mile radius from the prison and found the only available spaces were in Offord Road, five minutes' walk from the jail. Brilliant, he thought; the only downside was the cost - £16.70 for two hours.

'Jesus Christ,' he muttered, but had no choice. He did not want to park too far away in case his leg gave him problems, and so had very little choice. Small wonder that there were seven free spaces on that stretch of road. Seventeen pounds for two hours: that was just over fourteen pence per minute.

He reluctantly paid and booked the space, then resumed his journey, stopping off for a sandwich on the way. He arrived at the prison gates fifteen minutes before the appointment time and went through the same process as before.

There was a look of recognition and confusion on Jaylon's face as Jack joined him at the table.

'Where's my mother?' he asked as Jack sat down. 'Is she all right?'

'She's fine; nothing to worry about. I needed to speak to you some more, and she agreed that I could come in her place. She'll be here tomorrow.'

Jaylon nodded. 'You want to ask me more things?'

'Yes. I've been looking at the boy who died; you know, to try to piece together who would want to kill him. Did you know him? I probably asked you that before.'

'I told you, no. The first time I saw him was in that fighting on the Green.'

'Does the name Levi mean anything to you?'

There was a very slight pause as if Jaylon was thinking about the name. 'No, nothing.'

'What about Loki?'

'I told you, I don't know any of those names.'

'Not even Loki in those movies?'

'Oh, yes. In that TV show as well.'

'Apart from there, you don't know anyone called Loki? What about Tony?'

'Who's Tony?'

'Another guy, a bit older than Levi.'

'No.' As he replied, Jayon shook his head, looking down at the table.

'What about guys posing as homeless people outside supermarkets? You know, sitting on the ground in a sleeping bag, plastic cup out for money? Not really being on the streets, just using that as cover for money laundering?'

Jaylon gave a nervous laugh. 'No, never heard of that.'

'Apart from your mother, has anybody else been in contact with you here?'

'Just my solicitor.'

'Not your brother?'

'No, Mum just passes on what he says.'

'What he says?'

'Just things like, "Jamal says hello and he hopes you are okay."'

'Nobody else?'

'Only you.'

'Apart from me.'

Jaylon shook his head, saying nothing.

'And all the stuff I've just told you – about Levi, Loki, and the stuff with the supermarkets – it all means nothing to you?'

Jaylon shook his head again.

'Okay,' said Jack. 'Look, I'm trying to find out as much as I can about Navindra Dhabi, the boy who died. I'm trying to find out who would want to kill him.' He paused a second. 'Unless it was something unplanned, spontaneous during that fight. So it might not be murder if it wasn't planned.'

'What would it be then?'

'Possibly manslaughter. Has your solicitor spoken to you about that?'

'I don't think so. He just said he'll deal with everything. He said he's got a meeting with the judge.'

'Hm. And you still have no memories of how you came to be holding the murder weapon right next to his body?'

'No. Sorry.'

'There's no need to apologise. And you're not - or weren't – taking any drugs yourself?'

'No,' Jaylon replied, shaking his head.

'And you weren't having sex with men around your age or maybe a little bit older?'

'No, definitely not. Nothing like that.' Jaylon glanced around; then, lowering his voice, added, 'Never had sex before. Not with someone else, I mean.'

'Okay, okay,' said Jack. 'I was just clutching at straws. I think I'm done here. Have you got any messages for your mother or brother?'

'Just that I'll see her tomorrow.'

'Is there anything you need, you want her to bring?'

'No, nothing. No, wait – could you ask her to bring a few of my Batman comics?'

'No problem. How many? Any particular ones?'

'The last two or three. Just to… you know.'

A prison guard stepped over and began to lead Jaylon out. As he left, Jack said, 'Take it easy,' regretting it as soon as he spoke. A way of saying goodbye, but not appropriate in the circumstances.

He waited until Jaylon had left the hall, then stood to leave. Another officer led Jack to the double swing doors. He could not wait to get out of the prison; it was just as depressing as before.

He got home just after five. The leg was fine. He was relieved that he was okay to drive once more. He cooked himself some pasta, and sat down with it and a bottle of Heineken. It had been a long day, his first without the painkillers.

While eating, he took out the copy of the *Metro* he had picked up when he stopped off for petrol. He would do this regularly in place of his own paper, feeling it was useful to see what the competition were doing.

The outer pages comprised an advertisement feature, today about new build apartments near Chelsea Harbour. A bit irritated, he flicked the page over to what he called the proper front page, which tonight was devoted to another Westminster scandal, this time about one of the political parties' donor being accused of racist language, and the Prime Minister's desperate attempts to justify not returning the fifty thousand pounds he had donated.

He quickly flicked the page over. His eyes caught one headline on Page Two.

It was about the murder of a thirty-two year old man, named Anthony Carpenter.

Anthony.

Tony.

The picture was of a work identification badge. Not a good picture, but it was unmistakeably of the person Jack had spoken to on Friday

It had happened again.

Somebody was found murdered after speaking to Jack.

Just like Levi.

Only this time was much worse.

CHAPTER THIRTY-FOUR

Tony had been found by a neighbour, in his bedroom. He had been badly beaten up, and several of his fingers had been broken. There were also signs of sexual assault.

Much to Jack's relief, the police were looking for two men. A neighbour had heard loud noises coming from Tony's flat, and saw two men leaving the building. The report also showed a poor definition screen shot from a camera view of the entrance doors. Two figures, both dressed in hoods, which were pulled up, making it virtually impossible to make out their faces, were leaving the building.

Shit, Jack thought, *I was there the other day.*

The question now was, what should Jack do?

There were two factors here. Firstly, two people who had spoken to Jack had been murdered. The bogus invitation to Limehouse was obviously an attempt to get hold of him, so he would also be found floating in Limehouse Basin. He was not quite so concerned about himself: he was much bigger than Levi and Tony, and could also handle himself quite easily, as he did when he was stabbed. Plus, whoever was behind the killings had no idea where Jack lived, only where he worked; they may not even know that.

The bigger question was about whether the time had come for him to go to the police. The last thing he wanted was for the police to go steaming in and arrest everybody in sight, shutting down his own lines of enquiry. On the other hand…

He decided he would sleep on it himself, and run it past Mike Smith in the morning.

'Bloody hell, Jack: what have you got yourself into now?'

Mike's reaction was as Jack had expected. After sleeping on it, Jack's feeling was that he should go to the police. He didn't actually want to, for the reasons he had always felt; but there was always the risk of things going pear-shaped if he didn't. Mike was his get out of jail free card - not literally, hopefully – as if he said he didn't feel Jack should go to the police, then fine, Jack was only following his supervisor's instructions.

'I just need your input, Mike. Two people have been murdered after I've spoken to them. Should I go to the police with what I know?' He hoped Mike would give him a straight answer now; not some prevarication, like he needed to talk to the paper's management or lawyers first.

'What do you know? Do you know much?'

'Not a hell of a lot, but I'm getting there.'

Mike gave a long sigh: this was a sure sign that he was having to think on his feet. He didn't want to say he would consult, as in his position of News Editor, he should be able to come to that decision himself; but he didn't like being put in a position where he had to make that kind of decision. There were a few moments' silence, then he spoke.

'Look, Jack: I think you have to go to the police with what you know. Yes, I suppose you could argue that there's nothing you have that they need, and I'm guessing that they have worked out that the two murders are connected. And they have the video footage of the two guys entering and leaving the flat.'

'But they don't know that they are probably the same two who tried to meet me in Limehouse.'

'Quite. So yes, I think you should share it with them. Of course, there's always the risk that – well, if you were to unsee that footage and you know, be unaware of the two murders – you only read about them online, didn't you? Nobody actually told you. If you did take that view, and these murders end up all over the news, it would be crap publicity for the paper if it came out that one of our reporters withheld information from the authorities. And I think that you have a moral obligation to go to the police. They've made an appeal: you have information, and so you should share it with them. It can hardly screw up what you're doing, can it?'

'Only if the guys in the hoods are already known to them, and they pick them up. Then that could be my story killed.'

'Oi just changed. Another angle. This doesn't affect the kid who was arrested, does it?'

'No, I suppose not,' Jack conceded. It did occur to Jack that he was in danger of being sidetracked, of losing the focus on Jaylon Soji.

'There's another aspect you should consider,' Mike said. He was on a roll now. 'That's the question of *quid pro quo*. They might be prepared to share information with you.'

'Yes, I was thinking about that.'

'So that's settled, then. Do you know who's dealing with it?'

'The news report included an appeal from a detective inspector - I can't remember the name - working out of Islington nick.'

'Islington,' Mike repeated slowly. 'I don't know anybody from over there. I'll leave you to call them, then. Keep me up to date with how you get on, won't you?'

'I will.'

After ending the call, Jack checked the news article. The appeal was by a Detective Inspector Tyler, from Islington Police Station. A number was given for any information. Jack called the number.

Jack stated that he was calling about information regarding the murder of Anthony Carpenter, and was eventually put through to a woman who introduced herself as Detective Sergeant Jones.

'What type of information do you have?' Jones asked.

Jack explained who he was, and the story he was working on.

'Two of the people I have spoken with have been murdered. I don't think it is a coincidence.'

'Two? Who is the other?'

'A boy called Levi - I'm afraid I don't remember his surname – who was found in Limehouse.'

'I'm aware of that case,' she said. 'My colleagues working out of Limehouse Station will be working that. Look: we appreciate you getting in touch. My supervisor will want to talk with you: are you able to get down here?'

'Is that Detective Inspector Tyler?'

'It is, yes.'

'I'm in Cockfosters right now; I could be in Islington by twelve.'

'I'll just check he'll be available then.' There was a pause, then she returned. 'Could we say twelve thirty?'

'Twelve thirty is good for me.'

'We're in Tolpuddle Street. Just go to the front desk and ask for the Detective Inspector.'

'Will do. See you twelve thirty.'

So it was back to Islington, he thought. He would take the tube: the drive would be horrendous this time of day. He was also inclined to check out Tony's place while he was back down there; maybe talk to the neighbours. Maybe check out that 7/11 again. That would probably have to wait until after he had spoken to the police. Maybe Mike was right: there could be an opportunity for a bit of mutual back scratching here. If he helped them, they might be inclined to share with him, on the record and off.

He stood up and tested his leg. It seemed fine. There hadn't been the need for any painkillers for a day or so – things were going in the right direction there.

It was then that he realised Mike hadn't asked him about his leg. Jack snorted.

Par for the course.

CHAPTER THIRTY-FIVE

IN THE ENGLISH county of Dorset, between the towns of Poole and Dorchester, is the village of Tolpuddle, famous for the story of the Tolpuddle Martyrs.

In 1834, six agricultural workers were convicted of swearing an oath in secret as members of the Friendly Society of Agricultural Labourers. They were arrested and charged under the Unlawful Oaths Act of 1812 during a labour dispute over reduction of wages and were transported to a penal colony in Australia. After mass protests of over ten thousand people, they were pardoned in 1836 and returned to England three years later. The martyrs became a popular cause for early workers' rights and union movements.

Formerly going by another name, the thoroughfare was named Tolpuddle Street in 1986 to mark the 150th anniversary of a dinner held to celebrate the remission of the martyrs' sentences. The Islington tunnel of the Regent's Canal lies directly beneath Tolpuddle Street. In the nearby Copenhagen Fields, there is a plaque commemorating the martyrs.

Jack put his phone down and leaned back in his seat. On his way down to Islington, he spent part of the journey online, researching the etymology and history of the street. He had heard of the Tolpuddle Martyrs, had no idea where Tolpuddle was, and had not realised that was the origin of the Trade Union movement. If he had time, he would take a detour to Copenhagen Fields to check out that plaque. Now there was another point: why Copenhagen Fields? There was a Copenhagen Tunnel just outside Kings Cross station. Were they connected, and what was their history?

He came out of his reveries as he noticed his train was pulling into Kings Cross St Pancras station. A quick change onto the Northern Line, then one stop to Angel.

The police station was at number two

Tolpuddle Street. A brown-bricked, three-storey building dating from the thirties, it looked as if it had been recently refurbished, the brickwork façade cleaned. The doors were in a covered recess, almost a small *porte cochere*, access to which was through one of the three tall narrow arches. A police car was parked outside.

Inside, Jack walked up to the front desk. A uniformed officer was talking with an elderly man. English was clearly not the man's primary language, and they were having difficulty understanding each other. The plexiglass screen was not helping. Jack stood and waited patiently, studying the numerous community policing notices on a board on the wall.

Eventually, another officer appeared at the desk.

'Can I help you, sir?'

'Yes, my name's Jack Richardson. I'm here for an appointment with Detective Inspector Tyler. Twelve thirty.'

The young officer's eyes darted up to the wall clock, which read twelve twenty-six. 'Take a seat, Mr Richardson. I'll tell the DI you're here.'

Jack sat down on one of the six uncomfortable blue plastic seats. At exactly twelve thirty, a door opened, and a man stood in the doorway. He was of average height, looked around forty years of age, with receding greying hair. 'Mr

Richardson?'

'Yes.' Jack stood up and walked over, shaking Tyler's outstretched hand.

'DI Tyler. Come this way, please.'

Tyler led Jack to an interview room and gestured for him to sit down. 'You called,' he said as they both sat, 'to say you had information regarding Anthony Carpenter.'

'That's correct.'

'When you spoke to Sergeant Jones, you said you were a reporter. The *Daily News*?'

'That's correct. Tony Carpenter was involved in a story I'm working on. Look – I brought my notes in for you to read, but they're on a flash drive. Do you have anything to read this on?'

Tyler stood up. 'I'll go get something.'

He left Jack alone in the room for a couple of minutes before returning with an open laptop. While he was alone in the room, Jack noticed Susan had messaged him earlier that morning to ask how he was doing. He would reply once he was finished here.

'May I?' Tyler held out his hand.

'Sure.' Jack passed him the drive and watched while Tyler opened up the file and read it. After a few seconds, Tyler said, 'So, you're working on a story about a Jaylon Soji.' He paused and looked over at Jack. 'I know that name. But he pleaded guilty, and is awaiting sentencing, if I remember rightly. What's the nature of what you're working on?'

Deciding discretion was the better part of valour and it was probably not a good idea to even suggest that Jaylon might not be guilty, he replied, 'A kind of human interest piece. You know – the background to the killer and to his victim.'

'And how was that connected to Anthony Carpenter?'

'Well, for a start, there have been two murders.'

'Two?'

'Yes, the other day. A kid by the name of Levi. I don't know his surname. He was found floating in Limehouse Basin.'

'Limehouse? Yes,' said Tyler. 'I'm aware of that. The team at Limehouse Station will be dealing with that. You're saying that could be connected with Carpenter?'

'If it's not, it's one hell of a coincidence. In both cases, I talk to them, within a day or so, they're murdered.'

'Can I see your hands?' Tyler asked.

With a quizzical look on his face, Jack held out his hands, palms up. Tyler reached out and turned Jack's hands over, knuckles up. 'Why? Oh, I see. No, I didn't kill him.'

'Just routine, thank you,' said Tyler. 'Getting

back to what's on this USB stick, you've been looking at the lifestyles of both killer and victims, and you came across all this?'

'Yes. Navindra Dhabi, the first victim. He was in a gang, the E8 gang. It seems they were laundering proceeds of various crimes, extortion and blackmail, amongst other things.'

Tyler nodded slowly as he read what was on his screen. 'Married men with rent boys?'

'It would seem to be the case. Plus drugs. Their method of distribution is all in those notes.'

'Yes,' said Tyler as he glanced down at his screen. 'Posing as homeless people outside supermarkets.'

'So ubiquitous they're almost invisible.'

Tyler nodded. 'It says here about going to a meeting in Limehouse the other night.'

'Yes, the message was from the boy Levi's phone. I'd already read that he was dead, so I knew the message was bogus.'

'So you went along anyway?'

'Not to meet them, but to, well… observe them. And I'm certain - I only saw them from a distance, in the dark – they were the same two who were on that CCTV going into and coming out of Carpenter's flat.'

'You knew this meeting was bogus, a trap, maybe; but you went along?'

'To see who had sent the message.'

'And you never thought of contacting us?'

Jack felt awkward. Like a little boy in front of the headmaster. 'Well, maybe I should've; but that was only my theory.'

'You could have put yourself in danger. It says here about you being attacked yourself.'

'Yes, I was looking around where Navindra Dhabi lived, and I was attacked by two men. Different men, different build. One of them stabbed me in the leg.'

'It's obviously okay now. What did you do?'

'I broke his nose. The other one ran off.'

'Again I ask: you never thought of reporting this assault? You realise that if your broken nose man reports it, you could be charged with assault yourself?'

'Is he likely to report it? And where's the evidence?'

Tyler said nothing.

'You've read my notes – you can keep the flash drive, by the way. It's a copy I made for you. Is there anything else you want to ask me?'

Tyler took a deep breath. 'Not at the moment. We'll need to study this and see if it matches with our investigations. Of course, we'll have to liaise with the Limehouse team. As they say, don't leave town.'

'Don't worry: I won't. Can I ask you something?'

'Go ahead.'

'I've given you access to all my work. *Quid pro quo* – anything you can share with the press?'

'Not at the moment. Don't worry, I'm not being bloody minded. Our investigations are in the early stages. What you've give us here will be helpful.'

'So there's nothing you can tell me?'

'It seems you know more than we do.'

'What about Tony Carpenter? How was he killed?'

Tyler sighed again. 'Off the record: one of his neighbours heard noises coming from his flat. He saw the two men leave. They failed to shut the door properly, so the neighbour was able to get access. He found Mr Carpenter's body. In his bedroom.'

'Stabbed, or what? Presumably not shot.'

'He'd been systematically tortured and beaten to death. That's why I checked your hands. He had bruising about everywhere. Burn marks on his arms. Four of his fingers were broken. He had also been sexually assaulted.'

'How?'

'When he was found, his face and clothing were covered in blood. He had been wearing a pair of shorts; these were pulled down to his knees. He had been penetrated. Both *pre-* and *post-mortem.*'

'Sounds like they were enjoying it. You have semen, DNA, then?'

Tyler shook his head. 'A beer bottle was found near his body. The blood on the neck of the bottle matched his. You said they must have enjoyed it: well, Mr Richardson, you're probably right. The bottle was unopened. There were two matching bottles in his refrigerator. So, it's likely they went looking for something to use.'

'Jesus,' Jack said through gritted teeth.

CHAPTER THIRTY-SIX

IT WAS EARLY afternoon when Jack left the police station. Apart from DI Tyler's lurid description of what had happened to Tony Carpenter, and how he died, there was very little Jack had got out of talking to the police. Maybe a vague statement that they would share any relevant information with him, if they felt it appropriate. That was a big get-out clause – *if* they felt it appropriate. In other words, forget it. But he had done the right thing – *fulfilled his legal and moral obligations*, as Mike Smith had put it. At least the paper was off the hook if the shit hit the fan; after all, that was what Mike was interested in.

The message from DI Tyler was quite clear: by all means do what you need to do for the purposes of your newspaper and your article, but don't play detective. He had already been assaulted once – it could be worse next time. That was another thing which got under Jack's skin: Tyler seemed more concerned about Jack's 'assault' on the other man, the man with the broken nose, the man who stabbed Jack, than he was about the actual stabbing.

Tyler's last words as he let Jack out were: 'Remember, if you get any new information, I'd be obliged if you'd share it with us. We'll reciprocate if we feel it relevant and appropriate.'

Jack started to walk down the street when his phone pinged.

'Oh, shit,' he said aloud, when he saw who the text was from. He called Mike Smith back immediately.

After Jack had briefed him on the conversation with the police, Mike asked, 'So what are you going to do now?'

'Well, *now*, I'm going to get myself something to eat and go for a piss. Not necessarily in that order.'

'When you've done that.'

'I'm not sure. So far, everyone I speak to seems to get murdered. When I spoke to Tony at his place not too far from here -'

'Is he the first or second?'

'He's the second. According to the detective I spoke to, he wasn't just murdered; he was tortured and raped with a beer bottle.'

'Fuck.'

'Precisely. He told me he used to get his stuff - the drugs he was trading in - from a convenience store on the main road here. I'm thinking about starting there.'

'Starting by doing what?'

'I might do some shopping there, have a longer look around. See if I can provoke a reaction from someone, someone else I can talk to.'

'Be careful, for Christ's sake.'

'I will.'

'In the meantime, I do need some copy from you.'

'Yeah, sure. When by?'

'Yesterday would have been good.'

'Okay, fair enough,' Jack sighed. 'I'll just take a look at that 7/11 first, while I'm down here; then I'll get back and put something together. Something by way of an introductory piece; "more to follow", that kind of thing.'

'I need at least five thousand words, bare minimum. Have you written anything about the trial itself yet?'

'No, because there wasn't a trial. He changed his plea to guilty at the last minute.'

'So…' There was a long pause, which meant that Mike was thinking on his feet. '…you could approach it something on the lines of the suspect had pleaded guilty and is awaiting sentencing, pending reports. You could get some stats on teenage murders.'

'The victim was nineteen, yes. And the other two were a bit older.'

'Mid-twenties, then. Murdered in the last five years. London and the whole UK. Stats on victims, and of killers. Get a picture of the victim and the killer, from the family and the police mugshot. That will fill up some space. You could look at trends over the last five, ten years. London and countrywide. Are the figures going up or down? What could be impacting on that? You know the sort of thing I mean.'

'Okay, Mike. I'll be back home around three. I'll start putting something together once I get back. Five thousand minimum. Then I'll upload it this evening. Will that be okay?'

'I'll need it by noon tomorrow, so it gets in the next paper edition. Cheers, Jack.'

With that, Mike ended the call. While they had been speaking, Jack was walking in the direction of the convenience store.

When he arrived, he looked around the parade of shops. All looked clear: no characters in hoodies. He stepped inside, immediately behind a woman with two young children. The cashier was the same man as there had been before. He was serving a man who was dropping off a package for collection. Jack began browsing the shelves, slowly walking down the first aisle. He was certain he was on CCTV, but who was watching, if anybody? The cashier would have a monitor, probably one of those split screen images; Jack wondered if whoever was upstairs was watching, too.

He made his way to the back of the store and switched aisles. The door to the stairs was open again, but today a multi-coloured beaded curtain hung, obscuring the view.

There was nothing to see here: Jack speculated that the cashier noticed him follow Tony out of the store, and raised the alarm, prompting the other two to follow. They had to have been waiting upstairs.

He was in the confectionery aisle: picking up a bar of chocolate, he took his place at the till, behind two other people. When it was his turn, he held out the chocolate for the cashier to take and scan, and stared the cashier in the eye. Their eyes locked, and it took a couple of seconds for the cashier to recognise him. Jack paid for the chocolate, gave the cashier a broad smile, and left the shop.

Once outside, he paused a few seconds, and

went back into the shop. As he expected, the cashier was on the phone. A customer was waiting. He froze as Jack stopped in the doorway and looked at him. Jack shook his head, made a tutting sound, and left the store again. Once outside he hurried up the street. The store at the very end of the parade was a charity shop: Jack stepped inside, and positioned himself in the middle, ostensibly perusing nick-nacks, but watching out of the window. He was partially hidden by a rack of coats.

After two or three minutes, two figures walked past. Both had hoods around their head. One was grey, the other black: Jack could not recollect the colours in the CCTV image, and at Limehouse it was dark, but the two men's builds gave them away. They were walking quickly, as if in pursuit.

Jack peered out of the door, and could see them further up the street. He took off his coat, and carried it under one arm as he walked briskly across the road and in the direction of the tube station. Another theory proved correct.

He continued his brisk pace as far as Angel station. As he stood on the escalator taking him down to the platforms, he realised he had forgotten to go over to Copenhagen Fields to check out the Tolpuddle Martyrs plaque.

CHAPTER THIRTY-SEVEN

SETTLED IN AT home, Jack booted up his laptop and began. He decided to follow Mike's suggestions, so there was some online research he had to do first.

After around an hour of searching, he had assembled some figures. He jotted them down in tabular form, although they would not appear in this format in the article.

He went back five years, and put together the averages of under thirties killed per year, for Greater London, and the country as a whole. He then repeated that for the same age bracket convicted of murder. In both categories, the figure for London was around eighty percent of the nationwide figure.

Seventy-two percent of the victims were male; this figure was ninety-seven percent in the case of those convicted. Although Jack had chosen to document annual averages, he could see that the figures had been incrementally rising year on year, this trend pausing only in the pandemic years. None of these statistics surprised Jack, and would probably not surprise anyone else.

For the headshots that Mike had requested, Jack went to the *Daily News* archive, where thumbnails were already on file, from when the murder was first reported and when Jaylon Soji was first charged.

Jack sat back, stretched, yawned, and re-read what he had typed. He sighed and shook his head. He was not a hundred percent satisfied, and would have liked to have spent more time on this. However, as he was told once: less investigating, more writing.

This was why he hated having deadlines. With this type of story, any deadline was artificial; it could always be kept till the next day. Or the day after. Best to wait until the finished article was ready, as opposed to an arbitrary deadline which meant that what he sent in would be little more than a rough draft.

But, Mike Smith was Jack's Editor, and so he

had little choice. Once he had typed the last sentence, he read through the whole piece. Then read through it again, after which he went and made himself a cup of coffee. Then he read the piece one more time.

That done, he sent Mike Smith an email to say he had finished the article, adding, "I hope this is satisfactory" before clicking on the UPLOAD button. Breathing a sigh of relief, he pushed his laptop away and finished his coffee.

Now he had finished that, and hopefully got Mike off his back for a few days at least, he had to decide on his next course of action.

As he was typing the article, he was minded to send a message to Levi's phone, suggesting another meet. It would undoubtedly be the two hooded guys who picked up, and equally undoubtedly they would know that he was aware he was not talking to Levi. Then he thought again: what purpose would that serve?

No, the next logical step would be to concentrate on Tony's murder. When he first learned of the murder, there was a quotation from one of the neighbours, so it would be worthwhile making yet another trip down there, to visit where Tony lived and talk to the neighbours.

Once decided, he checked if there was a reply to his email. Seeing there was not, he switched off the laptop, threw the rest of the coffee away, and went to bed.

He was asleep within five minutes.

CHAPTER THIRTY-EIGHT

BACK DOWN TO Islington, once more leaving the car at home.

From reaching the top of the Angel station escalators, to walking through the station foyer onto Upper Street, and heading in the direction of Tony's flat, Jack's eyes were constantly darting around, looking for two men in hoodies.

It did strike him, as he crossed the road by the Green, that all the men had to do was either be on their own, or dress differently, and Jack would never recognise them.

Nevertheless, he kept alert, especially in the vicinity of Tony's block of flats.

He reached the flats, and double checked the vicinity. No hooded couple; police presence, either. Obviously, the police had finished here.

Still looking around but endeavouring not to look suspicious, he walked up to the door. He was unsure which of the door buttons to press, and the report quoted one of the neighbours, but gave no name.

At the bottom of the column of button was the one marked TRADES. He pressed that, and the lock clicked loudly, and he was able to push the door open. As easy as that, he thought. Unbelievable.

Usually in a small block like this one, there was somebody, normally a man, who knew everything that was going on, all the comings and goings. He would normally be older, normally retired. If he was younger, he would probably come over as nerdy. He would be the first in line for any interview or quotation to the press. He would normally occupy one of the flats nearest to the doors, so he could see who was coming and leaving. There was a set of windows either side of the entrance, and Jack would bet that this person lived on one of those flats. In fact, he had probably been watching Jack standing outside working out which button to press.

As he stepped inside, Jack saw that the first door on the left was Flat 1 and the first on the right was Flat 6. He was just about to head for Tony's flat when the door to Flat 6 opened. A man emerged: small, white hair but balding. Jack guessed early seventies. As he had expected, a retired man.

'Can I help you?' the man asked.

'Um, okay. I'll come quietly,' said Jack as he handed the man one of his business cards.

'Oh, you're from the press?' He seemed interested. 'You want to ask me some questions? I take it you're here about young Tony.'

'I am, yes. And I would like to talk to you, Mr...?'

'Brennan. Walter Brennan. As in.'

'As in?'

'The actor. Walter Brennan.'

'I'm not sure I've heard of him.'

'Before your time, young man. You want to come inside?'

'Surely,' said Jack, following Brennan inside.

'Take a pew,' Brennan said. 'Yes, my old man loved cowboy films, as he called them. So named me after one of the stars of them. Now, you wanted to talk about poor Tony.'

The first thing that struck Jack was that he was in the home of a single man. Everything functional, no embellishments. Much like his. The place seemed tidy, and clean. There was an impressive TV on the wall which had to have been at least sixty-five inches. Jack was impressed. Neatly piled on a table in the window bay were newspapers, probably one of each. He could tell by the front page and the state of them that they were that day's. So that was what Brennan did all day: look out of the window and read every newspaper. Jack wondered if he was lonely. Single or widowed? Probably a bachelor.

'Yes. Tony.'

'That was so awful. So tragic.'

'How well did you know him?' Jack asked.

'Off and on. Off and on. He was always going out, to work, I suppose. Not sure what he did. We used to pass on the corridor outside. He used to have a lot of visitors, as well. Men. None of my business, of course. His flat is directly above here, and if I was in my bedroom, I'd often hear things.'

'What sort of things?' As he asked, Jack knew the answer.

'Well, let's say noises. Thumping. Creaking. You get what I'm talking about?'

'I get it. The day his murder was reported, there was a CCTV image of two men in hoods leaving.'

'That's right. There's always people coming and going. The police must have got the CCTV from the owners of the building, and I supposed those fellas looked suspicious.'

'And the time they came and went would have tied in with the approximate time of death.' Jack decided not to volunteer the fact that he had visited Tony himself the other day.

'I suppose so,' Brennan went on. 'I saw them arrive, I think. I could see two figures standing at the door. They looked a bit shady, so I stood back a bit so they couldn't see me. I could hear voices, and I thought I could hear Tony's coming from the speaker out there. Then I heard the lock click like I did with you. It's quite loud. I heard them come in, then go up the stairs. After five minutes or so I heard noises coming from the bedroom. Not like normal, though.'

'Not like normal? How do you mean?'

'Different sorts of noises. Not like the sound of his bed creaking. Louder, too. I thought I could hear Tony cry out. That used to happen a lot, but not like this. Then it all went quiet. Then I heard the men leave.'

'Any other sounds? Voices?'

'I'll be honest with you: I did sit in the bedroom and listen. I could hear voices, yes; but I couldn't make out what they were saying. Then I heard Tony crying out.'

'Crying out anything in particular?'

'Just sounds; but that was quite common, as I said, if he had visitors.'

'Go on.'

'Like I say, they left and it went quiet. No sounds at all, which was strange. I used to hear him walking around. So I thought I'd better check he was okay. He had given me a key, just for emergencies. A lot of them here have done that. So I went up there. There was no answer when I knocked, so I let myself in.

'I found him in the bedroom. It was horrible. He was lying across the corner of the bed, on his front. His head was kind of hanging over the side of the bed. His face was covered in blood, and it was dripping onto the rug. His shorts had been pulled down to his ankles, and there was blood all over his arse.' Brennan silently mouthed the end of the sentence. 'He wasn't moving, so I called an ambulance. The police arrived just before the ambulance. I came back down here. The ambulance men took him away, then a couple of police officers came down to talk to me. I told them what I told you. They asked about his next of kin, but I didn't know anything about that. They stayed there around three or four hours, then left. Left with half a dozen black bags.' Brennan paused. 'Do you want to see his flat? I still have a key.'

Jack decided again not to divulge that he had

been here before, so checked himself before walking into the bedroom. 'Is it this way?' he asked.

Brennan nodded. 'That's where he was.'

The bed had been totally stripped. There was a dark stain on the mattress. The white rug which Jack recalled had gone.

'That's where I found him,' Brennan said. 'Lying across the bed.'

Jack sat down on the mattress and looked around. 'The police would have taken everything of any use. What's that?' he pointed at the keyring Brennan was holding.

Brennan looked down at the keyring. 'It's always been on there. One of those flashy drive thingies.'

'It is. And that's Tony's?'

'It is. And this is his door key.'

'Do you know what's on it?'

'I wouldn't know how to.'

'You got a computer?'

'I do, yes.'

'Could we have a look at what's on that?'

'Well, I suppose it couldn't hurt, seeing as he's dead.'

'The police didn't ask for it?'

'They don't know about it. I never thought much about it.'

'There's nothing left here. Can we go back to

yours and your computer?'

'You can, young man.'

Brennan's computer must have been at least twenty years old. Jack feared for a moment that it didn't have any USB ports, but it did, and they plugged in the drive.

It was filled with photographs. Tony appeared in most of them. They seemed to be holiday pictures: mainly beaches in sunny climes. He recognised some Parisian sights, and the canals of Amsterdam. Tony was usually with a male of similar age. Different location, different companions.

The locations turned to London. With Covent Garden in the background, there were pictures of Tony on his own, and some with yet another man. Then one picture caught Jack's eye. Still taken on the Covent Garden Piazza, it was a group selfie. Tony was at the side, and with him were Navindra Dhabi, with Levi, and Jamal and Jaylon Soji, all smiling at the camera.

CHAPTER THIRTY-NINE

FIVE PEOPLE.

Three of whom were now dead. Murdered.

Five people who, apart from the Soji brothers, apparently didn't know each other.

Jack pulled out his phone and took a picture of the photograph. Three times, for good measure.

'Thanks, Walter,' he said. 'I think I've got all I need.'

'You got any more questions you want to ask me?'

'Possibly, but I need to go somewhere first. I'll be in touch.'

'When will it be in the paper? You going to

quote me?'

'Not sure yet; I'll let you know.'

Jack left Brennan's flat and hurried back to the station. On his way back he debated whether to head back home and drive over to where he knew Jamal Soji would be, or use public transport. He paused in a shop doorway and checked an online planner. It would take thirty-five minutes to get there from where he was. There was no contest.

From Angel to Moorgate, then a short brisk walk to Liverpool Street, then on the Elizabeth Line to Ilford.

The journey actually took fifty minutes, but he would still arrive during the lunch peak, where hopefully he would catch Jamal.

On arrival, he walked over to the pizza store. There were no riders outside this time, so he walked into the store. A man in an apron was standing behind the counter. As soon as Jack entered the store the man asked, 'Can I take your order, please?'

'It's all right; I'm not here for a pizza. I'm looking for Jamal Soji.'

The man frowned. 'Nobody here with that name.'

'No, he's one of your riders. One of your delivery men.'

The man shrugged and shook his head, and held his hands out. Clearly, English was not his first language.

'It doesn't matter,' said Jack, turning and leaving the store. As he stepped onto the pavement, a delivery rider arrived. Jack watched as he parked and switched off the bike, got off, and started to take off his helmet. There was no recognition, so Jack gathered this was not Jamal.

Jack stepped over. 'Hi, sorry to bother you, but I'm looking for Jamal. Is he working today?'

The rider pulled a face. 'Jamal? Who's Jamal?'

'Jamal Soji. He's working as a delivery rider as well.'

It clicked.

'Oh, Jamal. Yes, I know him. No, he doesn't work here anymore.'

Shit.

'He's left?'

'U-huh.'

'When?'

'Yesterday, day before. Can't remember.'

'Where did he go?'

'Don't know. Sorry,' the rider said as he went into the store.

Jack looked around. He would need to go over to Jamal's home; hopefully he would be there, or at least his mother would know where he was. What a day not to have the car.

Fortunately, the station taxi rank had two cabs waiting, so Jack ran over, and took a taxi over to the Soji house. Mrs Soji answered the door.

'Mr Richardson,' she said. 'Come in, please.' He went in and followed her into the kitchen. This time, there was nothing on the stove. She turned to face him. 'Do you have good news about my Jaylon?'

Jack cleared his throat before replying. 'Actually, Mrs Soji, I've come to talk to Jamal. Is he around? They told me he's left his job at the pizza store.'

'I know he has; I don't know why. He's out at the moment. What do you want to talk to him about?'

Jack took out his phone and retrieved Photos. 'Mrs Soji, do you recognise anybody in this picture?'

She took the phone and stared at the photograph. 'Why, that's -'

'Leave her alone!'

Jack took the phone back from Mrs Soji and turned to face Jamal. He had just got home.

'No, Jamal…' she said, holding her arms out in a gesture of supplication.

'It's okay, Mama. Why don't you go for a lie down?'

'I'm all right,' she said, straightening down her clothing.

'Mama – go to your room. Go and have a lie down.'

Meekly, and saying nothing, she left the kitchen.

Before Jamal could speak, Jack held his phone out. 'Look at this picture. Tell me who's on it.'

'You already know who they are.'

'You tell me, Jamal.'

Jamal sighed. Resignedly, he said: 'Me and Junior, Tony Carpenter, Navindra Dhabi, Levi Maracar.'

'Do you know that, this one, this one, and this one, are all dead?' As he spoke, he pointed at Tony, Navindra, and Levi.

Jamal seemed surprised. 'No, but…'

'No, but - everything you told me earlier: that was all bullshit.'

'Where did you get that from?'

'From Tony Carpenter, indirectly. You want to tell me about it?'

Jamal leaned back against the stove. 'I take it you've found out what the gang does.'

'You mean the money laundering, distributing proceeds of crimes, the drug trafficking, the entrapment, the blackmail? The bogus homeless people?'

Jamal nodded. His bluster had gone.

'But you're not all in the same gang,' Jack said. 'Navindra and Levi were from the E8.'

'Doesn't always matter where money's concerned. The tall guy in the middle – Tony

Carpenter – he organises stuff locally. Tells everyone where to pick stuff up and drop it off. Used to send the younger ones out to meet up with old men scumbags. The second one would video it or take stills, then collect. He'd take a percentage of what the boys got. It seemed to work okay, then Nav and Junior fell out.'

'Fell out? How? Why?'

'Over the money. All of it – it's all about money. Junior and Nav would always split the dough fifty-fifty. After Tony had taken his cut, that is. But they had an argument about something, and Nav refused to hand over Junior's share.

'That night over at the Fields - when the shit hit the fan – Junior had got a text from Nav to say he was going to hand over his cut. That's why he came with us. There was lots of shit going on there – some fighting – but while all that was going on, Junior had planned to meet Navindra to get his money. But Navindra just told Junior to go fuck himself and that he was going to be partnering with Levi, whose own partner had just started a stretch for dealing. Junior lost it and killed him. Nav tried to get away, but Junior caught him in his stairwell. You know the rest.'

Jack closed his eyes while he processed this. Somehow, this revelation came as no surprise to him. Levi used to call himself Loki to conceal his identity. The last time Jack saw Jaylon, he switched to using the name Loki, and Jaylon didn't bat an eyelid, as if he knew Levi and Loki were the same person. At the time something didn't sit right; now he knew what it was. 'So he did kill Navindra after all?'

Jamal nodded. 'I told you he had a temper.'

'So, why the denial first, then claiming he can't remember anything?'

'He says he can't. Maybe he's fucking with you; maybe he genuinely can't remember. I told you: he's not normal. He can't process stuff like normal people.'

'Look,' said Jack. 'From what I know of his circumstances – and I'm sure that pending pre-sentencing reports, he'll be undertaking a bucketload of assessments – it's going to be commuted to manslaughter, under diminished responsibility. It was never premeditated: he didn't travel to London Fields with the sole intention of killing Navindra. That's going to be reflected in his sentence. He would probably end up not in a regular prison, but a lesser kind of facility.'

Jamal shrugged. 'What are you going to do now?' he asked.

'I'm going to try and finish my story, somehow. I don't think there's any need for me to see you again, or your mother, or your brother.

Somehow, I have to come to terms with the fact that two other people have been murdered as a result of all this. If I hadn't met up with them, they might still be alive.'

'I've an idea who might have killed them.'

'Who? Two guys in hoods?'

Jamal nodded. 'Tony spoke of two fellas who his boss used as kind of enforcers. Who did his dirty work. They were called William and Harry: you know, after... Not their real names; I think they were Polish, so nobody could say their names right, so gave them those monikers.' He paused a second. 'You going to the police?'

'Once I've finished my piece. There is stuff they need to know about. William and Harry need to be taken off the streets, and there's obviously something going on out of that convenience store in Islington. I think the police need to raid it.'

There was a few moments' silence when neither of them spoke. Eventually Jack broke the silence.

'Look, I'll leave you to it. Look after your mother. I'll let myself out.'

He walked past Jamal, out of the kitchen and down the hall to the front door. As he passed a closed door, he could hear Mrs Soji inside, sobbing. He rested a hand on the door handle, then stopped himself and left the flat. Outside on the street, he paused and took a deep breath of fresh air. He wanted to go home, but had no car, so he called an Uber to the station. While he waited, he decided he had a phone call to make before the car arrived.

A phone call and a text message, to be precise.

CHAPTER FORTY

JACK SHIVERED.

He was standing once again on the corner of Limehouse Causeway and Colt Street.

He checked the time. It read 20:56.

Four minutes to go.

Earlier, on his way home from the Soji house, he had retrieved Levi's number and sent a text.

Sorry about the other night. Sthg came up. Can meet u 2nite.

Within a minute, he got a reply.

OK same place as b4 make sure u show up

I will, promise, he replied.

Earlier, he had walked past the meeting point,

but there was nobody there. He waited around the block, out of sight.

A text came through just as the display changed from 20:59 to 21:00.

Wtf ru?

He replied, almost there, and began to walk. As he turned the corner, he saw, on the corner of the Causeway and Gill Street, a white van parked. A figure - hood down – was waiting on the pavement next to the van. As Jack got nearer, he saw the figure turn its head to the cab, and back again.

Jack stopped twelve feet away from the man.

'Where's Levi?' he asked.

Suddenly, a hand grabbed his right arm. Jack was big and he was strong, but this grip was firm. This was the second man, the Harry to the first man's William. He had got out of the driver's door and snuck around the van.

'Come meet Levi,' the man growled. He had a thick accent and he stunk of cigarettes, cheap sweet French ones.

Jack struggled again, and almost succeeded, until the first man stepped forward.

Then two cars pulled up, their blue lights illuminating the darkened street.

'Hold it there!' a voice called out.

'Cunt,' said the thick accented voice, momentarily loosening his grip.

'Fuck you too,' Jack snapped back, twisting his body to use the man's momentum to propel him into the other's.

'That's enough, Mr Richardson,' said Detective Inspector Tyler. 'We've got them now.'

Jack brushed himself down and looked over at Tyler.

'Nothing like leaving it till the last minute.'

'We were always there, sir,' said Tyler.

Jack nodded as William and Harry were bundled into the back of separate police cars, which then turned and drove away.

No blue lights this time.

CHAPTER FORTY-ONE

ONCE AGAIN, JACK used the *JustPark* app. This time he got a space a hundred yards up the same street from where he had parked before. This time it cost him £20.30 for two hours; last time he paid £16.70: he was perplexed as to why it should be different this time. Surely parking apps did not use dynamic pricing – he counted at least four unused spaces as he walked to the prison.

Forty-five minutes later, he was in the prison, filing into the Visitors Hall, where Jaylon and the other prisoners were waiting. Last time, all the tables were occupied; today there were three empty ones. Maybe today was a quiet day for visiting.

Jack gave Jaylon a brief nod as he sat down opposite him.

Jaylon spoke first. 'Have you found anything out?'

After his conversation with Jamal, Jack found his attitude to Jaylon had changed.

'Oh, yes,' he said. 'I've found plenty out.'

'To prove me innocent?'

'I think that ship's sailed, Jaylon.'

Jaylon looked puzzled. 'What do you mean?'

'I've been speaking to your brother. He told me what happened that night. You, and Navindra, and how you fell out. How you felt after Navindra shafted you for the money; how you lost it when he told you he was going to team up with Levi.'

Jaylon said nothing, staring at Jack, his eyes fixed on him, as if he was trying to read Jack's mind.

Then a grin came across his face: the first sign of any animation or emotion Jack had ever witnessed from him.

Then the grin left his face and he began rocking backwards and forward in his chair, making a grunting sound with each forward rock. Jack's eyes darted over to the guard by the wall, who had noticed what Jaylon was doing.

Then with a cry, Jaylon leapt out of the chair

and across the table at Jack, knocking the chair, Jack still in it, onto its back. It all happened in a second and Jack had not had time to react. Now Jaylon was sitting astride Jack, and started to pummel at him with his fists. Not punching him in the normal sense of the word, but doing the same thing a child having a tantrum does, thumping a table with its fists. Only here it was not a table, but Jack's face and head. His eyes were wide open and wild, the expression on his face almost feral. With each blow, he made those grunting sounds, but louder this time.

By now, Jack had had time to react and grabbed Jaylon's wrists, preventing him from raining any more blows. He was surprised how strong Jaylon was. Jaylon had time to land two or three blows before Jack could stop him, and before the guard was able to run over and pull the boy off Jack.

A second guard had come over, and they restrained Jaylon with a pair of handcuffs before leading him out of the hall. Jack could hear his cries as they took him down the passageway, back to his cell.

Jack lay on the ground, still connected to the chair, for a few seconds getting his breath back. The original guard was now by his side, helping him up.

'Are you all right, sir?' the guard asked.

'Yes, thank you,' replied Jack, who was now on his feet, brushing himself down. 'I'll live. Just took me by surprise, that's all.'

'Yeah, well,' the guard said, as he picked up Jack's chair. 'That one's got a temper, I can tell you. Sweetness and light and innocent one minute; the next... well, you saw that for yourself, didn't you?'

'I certainly did,' Jack said, looking over at the door through which they had taken a screaming Jaylon. 'I certainly did.'

CHAPTER FORTY-TWO

'YOU'VE FROZEN AGAIN, Jack.'

'No, you have. I can still hear you, though. Tell you what: let's hang up, and I'll call you back this time.'

Eventually Jack and Susan got their video call working. Jack had just explained what had happened at the prison.

'Are you okay? Shouldn't you be going to A&E?'

'A&E? What for?'

'To check your head out, give you a brain scan or something.'

'Jesus. If you think I'm going to make *two*

visits to A&E in a week... In any case, I didn't hit my head on the floor. My shoulders are a bit sore; they took all the impact.'

'No bones broken?'

'No. The prison doctor gave me a quick check-over before they let me leave. I'm fine, just a little sore. Just as well I have a supply of painkillers.'

'It's not funny. Anyway, so it was the boy in prison all along? He did kill the other kid?'

'It would seem that way, yes.'

'So what's your problem? That you were wrong?'

'His brother told me he was retarded, kind of special needs in politically correct terms. I don't necessarily buy that. You never saw his bedroom. Those model kits and stuff – so beautifully put together, crafted. Great attention to detail. So much creativity. It's hard to reconcile that with the kid I saw in prison today and what happened to the murdered one.'

'A split personality?'

'Something like that, maybe. It'll be included in the sentencing reports, they told me. And of course his medical and mental state will be taken into account when the judge decides his sentence. Then there were the other murders.'

'Yes, I'd forgotten about them. Wow, Jack: what a story. So all in all three murders?'

'Jaylon killed one, over an argument about money. The other two - Levi and Tony – were killed by those two jokers in the white van. William and Harry, as they were known by. But I still can't get it out of my head -'

'No, Jack. I know what you're going to say. None of the deaths were in any way your fault. Surely you can see that.'

'I know. That's what Cathy tells me.'

'And she's right. So, this kid Jaylon? He carries on waiting for reports, then sentencing. I suppose attacking you wouldn't have helped his case.'

'I doubt it.'

'And William and Harry? Surely they're not called that?'

'Nicknames, apparently. They're from Eastern Europe, and nobody can pronounce their real names. They've been arrested; out of harm's way now. There's no way they're going to get bail. They're probably in Pentonville with Jaylon. As for the others in the gang -'

'You mean those who stabbed you?'

'Including them. The one with the broken nose. They're still out there, I guess, unless they do a runner, scared Jaylon and William and Harry implicate them.'

'Will you be called as a witness?'

'Probably. I don't know when though. I'll

need to speak with the paper's legal people, to check what I can put in my article, because of the trial. A touch of the *sub judice*.'

'You'll be able to write something, though?'

'Of course; I'll just need to run it past the lawyers before it goes into print.'

Susan laughed.

'What?' Jack asked.

'I bet you've not even started it yet.'

'No, not yet. I was going to start tonight, but I'm exhausted. My back, head and leg hurt.'

'What do you expect? You were assaulted in a prison of all places, a few days after being stabbed. And what about those men who stabbed you?'

'What about them?'

'You said they're still out there. You will be careful, won't you, Jack?'

'I can look after myself; but yes: I'll be careful.'

'You look shattered.'

'I am shattered. Once we're done here, I'll just give Cathy a quick update. Then a long, hot bath, then sleep.'

'Best idea you've had in ages.'

*****

After taking his long, hot bath, Jack returned to the desk where his laptop rested. It was open, still on. The cursor was flashing, beckoning him.

He sat down.

Despite what he had said to Susan and Cathy, his mind was filled with the last few days' events. It would be a good time to start. While it was fresh in his mind.

He sat in silence for a minute.

His fingers hovered over the keyboard.

Then he shut the laptop and pushed it away.

Some things were best left for another day.

THE END

INTRODUCING LAPD DETECTIVE SAM LEROY...
LAST TO DIE

Los Angeles, late September, and the hot Santa Ana winds are blowing, covering the city with a thin layer of dust from the Mojave and Sonoran deserts.

That night, there are three mysterious, unexplained deaths. The official view is that they are all unrelated. The victims had no connection, and all died in different parts of the city.

However, Police Detective Sam Leroy has other ideas, and begins to widen the investigation. But he meets resistance from the most unexpected quarter, and when his life and that of his loved ones are threatened, he faces a choice: back off, or do what he knows he must do…

SAM LEROY RETURNS IN…

WRONG TIME TO DIE

'I don't think I've ever seen so much blood.'

When LAPD Detective Sam Leroy is called to a murder scene, even he is taken aback by the ferocity and savagery of the crime.

Furthermore, there seems to be no motive, which means no obvious suspects.

Believing the two victims themselves hold the key to their own murder, Leroy begins his investigations there, and before long the trail leads him to the island of Catalina, where a terrible secret has remained undiscovered for almost thirty years…

NO PLACE TO DIE

A severed head is found beneath the Hollywood Sign.

Fresh from wrapping his previous case, LAPD Detective Sam Leroy is called to the scene. Now he is tasked with identifying the victim and finding the rest of him. Not necessarily in that order.

Following up on the few leads they have, Leroy and his partner, Detective Ray Quinn, find themselves unravelling a complex puzzle, one which began two thousand miles from home, and which involves sex, extortion, and ultimately murder.

While Leroy follows the trail, he is feeling himself coming to the end of a relationship, and may possibly be making decisions he might later regret.

ANOTHER WAY TO DIE

Seven years ago, LAPD Detective Sam Leroy shot and killed Harlan Cordell, and breathed a sigh of relief that the reign of the infamous Pentagram Killer was over.

But now, the killings have begun again. The police believe they are dealing with some fanatical copycat, but these new murders share a small detail with those before, a detail only the police and the killer would know.

How can today's killer know the intimate details of seven years ago?

Or, as he fears, did Leroy kill the wrong man, leaving the real Pentagram Killer to wait and resume his grisly trade on an unsuspecting city?

READY TO DIE

In the middle of the night, a woman reports her husband missing. Soon after, his body is found by the side of Mulholland Drive, killed by a single bullet through the head.

When an adult movie executive is found shot, execution-style, LAPD Detective Sam Leroy and his partner Ray Quinn take on an investigation with minimal clues and no obvious suspects. Statistically, if a murder is not solved within forty-eight hours, it is likely to remain unsolved, and so they are in a race against time to find the killers.

Meanwhile, both men are each facing life-changing events, all of which conspire to make this case all the more challenging…

NO REASON TO DIE

Death on the streets. But who was the target?

Sam Leroy and his team are called to a 480 – a hit and run, which has left two dead and more injured.

It soon becomes a murder investigation when street cameras show the vehicle was driven deliberately onto the sidewalk.

Leroy looks at the case from two angles, one being to identify the vehicle and its driver, the other being the victims themselves, and who is most likely to be a target for murder.

One victim stands out from the rest: his personal and professional life suggest he is the most likely target, but when Leroy and his team begin to delve into the man's background, they find themselves in the murky world of politics, deception, and secrets.

ALSO BY PHILIP COX

THE VALUE OF NOTHING

A WET AUTUMN NIGHT
Newspaper reporter Jack Richardson lends his coat
and car to a friend

AN ACCIDENT
Within thirty minutes, Jack's car lies in flames

The crash seems suspicious, and Jack wonders if it
was an accident, or murder.

But if it was murder,
Who was the intended victim?

THE ANGEL

Investigative reporter Jack Richardson is assigned to a story involving sleaze and a prominent Member of Parliament.

During the investigation, Jack receives a call relating to an old case, one involving the murder of a twenty-year-old girl, suggesting that the case might not be as closed as everybody thinks.

Torn between his assigned story, and one where there might have been a terrible miscarriage of justice, Jack must make a choice.

His decision leads him into a dark place he never knew existed, and which puts him in great personal danger…

THE COYOTE

London newspaper reporter Jack Richardson is working on a story when he receives the news that his brother-in-law has been found dead in his car.

Having reservations about the verdict of suicide he starts to probe the circumstances, and finds similarities between his brother-in-law's death and the story he is working on, both connected to a chain of events which began three years earlier, and over a thousand miles away…

THE TRAIL

Tower Bridge, London

It is two in the morning, and a young student is seen diving off the bridge into the dark, icy waters below. When his body is recovered from the river, it is found to contain high levels of the drug Ecstasy.

The dead student shared a house with the niece of investigative newspaper reporter Jack Richardson, who decides to retrace the student's last few days to establish the true story behind his death.

However, as Jack follows this trail, he encounters dark forces, and a perilous outcome for both himself and his niece…

ALSO BY PHILIP COX

AFTER THE RAIN

Young, wealthy, handsome - Adam Williams is sitting in a bar in a small town in Florida.

Nobody has seen him since.

With the local police unable to trace Adam, his brother Craig and a workmate, Ben Rook, fly out to find him.

However, nothing could have prepared them for the bizarre cat-and-mouse game into which they are drawn as they seek to pick up Adam's trail and discover what happened to him that night.

DARK EYES OF LONDON

When Tom Raymond receives a call from his ex-wife asking to meet him, he is both surprised and intrigued – maybe she wants a reconciliation?

However, his world is turned upside down when she falls under a tube train on her way to meet him.

Refusing to accept that Lisa jumped, Tom sets out to investigate what happened to her that evening.

Soon, he finds he must get to the truth before some very dangerous people get to him…

SHE'S NOT COMING HOME

EVERY MORNING
At 8.30 Ruth Gibbons kisses her husband and son goodbye, and goes to work.

EVERY EVENING
At 5pm she finishes work, texts her husband leaving now, and begins her walk home.

EVERY NIGHT
At 5.40 she arrives home, kisses her husband and son, and has dinner with her family.

EXCEPT TONIGHT

SHOULD HAVE LOOKED AWAY

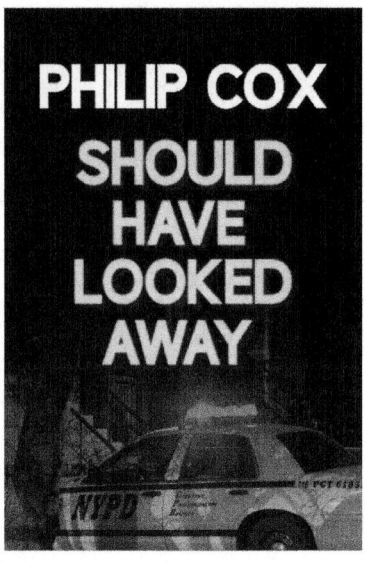

It began on a Sunday. An ordinary Sunday, and a family trip to the mall.

Will Carter takes his five-year old daughter to the bathroom, and there he is witness to a fatal assault on an innocent stranger.

Over the next few days, Will tries to put the experience behind him, but when he sees one of the killers outside his home, he becomes more and more involved, soon passing the point of no return.

Becoming drawn deeper and deeper into something he does not understand, Will feels increasingly out of his depth and is soon asking where this is going and was the victim as innocent as he first thought…

Printed in Great Britain
by Amazon